published by
Top Cow Productions, Inc.
Los Angeles

VOLUME 1

MARC BERNARDIN & ADAM FREEMAN • writers

AFUA RICHARDSON • artist

TROY PETERI • letterer

original editions edited by Betsy Gonia

Cover art by Afua Richardson & Nelson Blake II

for this edition, book production by Sasha Head

For Top Cow Productions, Inc.

Marc Silvestri - *CEO* • **Matt Hawkins** - *President and COO* • **Betsy Gonia** - *Managing Editor*

Elena Salcedo - *Operations Manager* • **Ryan Cady** - *Editorial Assistant* • *Vincent Valentine - Production Assista*

www.topcow.com

Genius Volume 1 Trade Paperback.
MAY 2015. FIRST PRINTING. ISBN: 978-1-63215-223-7. Printed in the USA.
Published by Image Comics Inc. Office of Publication: 2001 Center Street, 6th Floor, Berkeley, CA 947

PRELUDE

"WHAT I'M TRYING TO TELL YOU, SIR...
HENDRICKS
"...IS THAT WE'RE SITTING ON A POWDER KEG, JUST WAITING TO EXPLODE."

"I DON'T KNOW HOW LONG IT'S GONNA TAKE.
GLURGLE

DROP THE FUCKING GUN!
NOW!
POLICE

"OR WHAT'S FINALLY GONNA LIGHT THAT FUSE..."
HUG THE GODDAMN PAVEMENT!

NAH.
I DON'T THINK SO.

BUT WHAT I
DO KNOW, FOR
A FACT...
KRAK
KRAK
NOW, YOU LISTEN HERE... BITCH.
I'MA LET YOU PICK UP YOUR MEAT, HERE, AND CRAWL THE FUCK BACK FROM WHERE YOU CAME.
AND WHEN THEY ASS' YOU WHAT HAPPENED, YOU TELL 'EM. YOU TELL 'EM THAT THIS HERE BELONGS TO ME.
W-WHAT BELONGS TO YOU?
THIS NEIGHBORHOOD. 'S MINE. AND YOU AIN'T WELCOME NO MORE.
"...IS THAT IT'S COMING."

"IT'S COMING." YOU COME IN HERE ONCE A GODDAMN MONTH-- FOR THE LAST SIX YEARS--AND TELL ME ABOUT YOUR FUCKING POWDER KEG. I GOT NO TIME FOR THIS SHIT, GREY! WE ARE DROWNING IN REAL CRIMES.
LOOK, CAPTAIN. THIS IS NO GOOSE CHASE. THIS IS REAL--
A REAL WASTE OF FUCKIN' TIME. YOU GOT A PILE OF CASES ON YOUR DESK WIDER THAN MY WIFE'S ASS.
CAPTAIN
LOUIS HARDY
THUD
I AM A KID PLEADING WITH MY PARENTS TO BELIEVE THE MONSTER UNDER MY BED IS REAL.
ELEVEN YEARS WORTH OF DATA: DISSECTED, ANALYZED, CATALOGUED, AND CROSS-REFERENCED. IT ALL SUPPORTS ONE THEORY.
A THEORY TO WHICH ONLY I SUBSCRIBE.
DZELL
call mom
DETECTIVE REGINALD GREY
CLEAN ME!!!
"Suspect Zero"
COME OUT, COME OUT, WHEREVER YOU ARE...

YOU TWO CAN COME ON DOWN NOW.
GET G-TRON OUT HERE. TELL 'EM TO GET THIS BLACK N' WHITE OFF THE STREET AND RIG IT. WE GON' NEED IT LATER.
AND HAVE YOUR BRUH HACK ME INTO THEIR COMPUTER.
AIGHT, DEE. WE ON IT.
DESTINY... YOU SHOT DAT DUDE LIKE SHIT WAS PERSONAL.
IT WAS...
IT WAS THE END
GET EVERYONE TOGETHER. RIGHT HERE. RIGHT NOW.
WE GONNA HAVE US A GOOD OL' FASHION TOWN MEETING.

Y'ALL KNOW ME. YOU KNOW WHO I AM. I GREW UP ON THIS STREET. MY PARENTS DIED ON THIS STREET. HALF THE PEOPLE WE KNOW GOT THEMSELVES POPPED ON THIS FUCKIN' STREET...BY OTHER PEOPLE ON THIS FUCKIN' STREET. WHY?
THEY *WANT* US THIS WAY. WE A CANCER TO THEM, AND THEY HAPPY TO SIT BACK AND WATCH US EAT OURSELVES ALIVE.
FUCK. THAT.
SKELATAUR

I WANT A CRIB WITHOUT BARS ON THE WINDOWS. I WANT MY MAN TO DRIVE HIS CAR WITHOUT THE FIVE-O BUSTING HIS ASS FOR NOT BEING WHITE. AND THOSE ARE THE *GOOD* COPS.
I WANT A PLACE OF MY OWN. YOU WANT A PLACE OF YO' OWN.
LOTTA PUNKS 'ROUND HERE RUN THEIR MOUTHS. I DON'T TALK. *I DO.* WHILES BACK I ASKED YOU TO TRUST ME. I TAKE THAT SHIT REAL SERIOUS.
OUR TIME IS NOW.
SO HERE'S WHAT I'MA DO. DECLARE MARTIAL LAW IN THIS MOTHERFUCKER. NO MORE CALLING 9-1-1. *I'M* YOUR GODDAMN 9-1-1.
THIS PLACE BELONGS TO *US.* AND WE GON' KEEP IT.
LA

WE GOT A TEN-DOUBLE ZERO!

OFFICERS DOWN? WHAT HAPPENED?

S-SNIPERS. REAL PROS. T-TOLD ME TO...
DAMN IT, DANVERS, WHERE'S HENDRICKS? WHERE IS YOUR PARTNER?
S-SHOT... HE'S I-IN THE CAR.
THE CAR?! GET AN E.M.T. OUTSIDE--
HE DON'T NEED NO E.M.T. T-TRUST ME.

CAP, I KNOW DANVERS IS COVERED IN HIS OWN PISS, BUT HE'S TALKING ABOUT GANGBANGERS WHO GOT THE DROP ON TWO BUBBLEGUMS FILLED WITH VETERANS.
WITH SNIPERS.
FIVE MINUTES. IF THIS ISN'T FOR REAL, CONSIDER YOUR ASS BOUNCED.

MAKE IT COUNT, DETECTIVE.
OKAY. I'M NOT A SHARPSHOOTER, I'M LOUSY BEHIND THE WHEEL... MY THING IS DATA, PATTERNS, LOGIC--
I KNOW YOUR FUCKIN' RESUMÉ, REGGIE.
"RIGHT. OVER 35,000 REPORTED CASES OF GANG VIOLENCE OVER THE LAST DECADE.
BOOYAH
"THOUSANDS OF HOMICIDES, FELONY ASSAULTS, ROBBERIES, CARJACKINGS, KIDNAPPINGS, RAPES..."

"SEEMINGLY RANDOM AND CHAOTIC, YES. BUT EVEN IF THE UNIVERSE DOESN'T HAVE A DESIGN, IT DOES HAVE *ORDER*, CAPTAIN.

"CROSS REFERENCE EVERY CASE, EVERY VICTIM, EVERY PERP. TRIANGULATE LOCATIONS AND TERRITORIES, EXTRAPOLATE SUCCESSORS, CHAINS OF COMMAND, ALLIANCES, AND SO ON."
OFFICER JEMEL HORNE
COP SHOT IN DOWNTOWN DRUG BUST
WANTED DEAD OR ALIVE
FOR MURDER
ASSAULT WITH A DEADLY WEAPON.
ANY INFORMATION LEADING
TO ARREST OF THIS SUSPECT
WILL RESULT IN A REWARD OF
$10,000 PLEASE PROCEED WITH CAUTION
SUBJECT IS ARMED AND DANGEROUS.

Saratoga County
Juvenile Correctional Facility

...AND?

AND IT ALL LEADS TO ONE POSSIBLE OUTCOME.
WAR.

SOMEONE, A CENTRAL FIGURE, IS ORGANIZING THEM, TRAINING THEM, FOCUSING THEM AGAINST A COMMON ENEMY. US.
"I CALL HIM 'SUSPECT ZERO.'"
WON'T BE LONG NOW 'TIL THEY GET MY MESSAGE AND COME BACK HEAVY. YOU AIN'T A SOLDIER, THEN GIT.
IF YOU ARE A SOLDIER, WE GOT WORK TO DO. I NEED FLEETWOOD AND CAMARO SQUADS AT THE NORTH END OF THE STR--
AND WHAT IF I'S TIRED OF WORKIN' FOR YOU? WHAT IF I DON'T WANNA DIE FOR YOU?
WHAT IF I DON'T TRUST YOU?
WELL, THEN...
CRUNCH
KLAK
...YOU SHOULD'VE SHOT ME, 'DRE.
THIS IS WHAT Y'ALL WAITED FOR. THIS IS WHAT Y'ALL TRAINED FOR. THIS IS WHAT YOU WILL FIGHT FOR.
ANYONE ELSE GOT A PROBLEM?
THEN GET. TO. FUCKING. WORK.

I READ THIS BOOK ONCE ABOUT THAT CHESS KID, BOBBY FISCHER.

BOY SAID HE COULD SEE, LIKE, TWO OR THREE MOVES AHEAD 'A WHOEVER HE WAS PLAYIN'.

'THANK GOD,' I THOUGHT. 'I AIN'T NO FREAK.'

I AIN'T NO FREAK.
NAH, YOU AIN'T NO FREAK. TOO DAMNED SKINNY, THOUGH.
WHO GOT TIME TO EAT?

G-TRON GOT THE RC HOT AND READY.
GOOD. GOOD. THANKS, CHAVONNE.
YOU KNOW, DESTINY. IT ALWAYS FUCK WIT' ME WHEN YOU DO THAT SHIT WIT' YOUR VOICE.
WHEN YOU SOUND ALL... ALL WHITE 'N SHIT.
ONLY WITH YOU, GIRL. BECAUSE I TRUST YOU. BECAUSE YOU *KNOW.*
YOU KNOW WHY I'M DOING THIS.
BECAUSE, SO HELP ME, I DON'T KNOW HOW TO DO ANYTHING ELSE.

I DON'T KNOW, REGGIE...
ALL THE DATA IS THERE, YOU JUST HAVE TO KNOW HOW TO PROCESS IT.
Los Angeles Gang Territory
legend
"GANG-ON-GANG VIOLENCE IS DOWN. WHY? IT SURE AS HELL AIN'T US. AND THEY DIDN'T GET UP ONE DAY AND DECIDE TO PLAY NICE.
"NO. ONLY ONE THING UNITES ENEMIES...
POLICE
"A NEW ENEMY.
"YOU'VE GOT A LARGE GROUP OF WELL-ARMED PEOPLE, BRED INTO VIOLENCE, HARDENED IN BATTLE."
AND TODAY WE HAVE SNIPERS? TRIANGULATED CROSSFIRE?
HOODS. DISCIPLINED, METHODICAL... TRAINED.
LOU. THIS IS JUST *BEGINNING.*

GHT. UND FF. HUNDERBIRD?
YA HEAR?
FLEETWOOD.
YO.
CHARGER?
READY.
CUTLASS.
FUCKIN' ACCOUNTED FOR.
HOO-RAH.
WE GOT COMPANY.

S.W.A.T
EVERYBODY HOLD! DON'T DO SHIT!
CUTLASS, GET READY TO MOVE.
TO ALL ARMED PERSONNEL, YOU ARE ALL UNDER ARREST! DROP YOUR WEAPONS, STEP OUT IN THE OPEN AND HIT THE FLOOR!
S.W.A.T.
SPECIAL WEAPONS AND TACTICS
ABOUT TO STICK IT, DEE.

KRATTHOOM
S.W.A.T.
SPECIAL WEAPONS AND
NICE WORK, CUTLASS. BUT THERE SHOULD BE MORE BODIES.
FLEETWOOD. GIMME EYES ON THE ALLEY RUNNING PARALLEL TO THE DRAG.
GOT 'EM, DESTINY.
LIGHT 'EM UP.
LIT, BOSS.
TWIP
POK
ZIP
ZIP

WHAT THE FUCK?! FUCKING HELL!
BANG BANG
DON'T WASTE TOO MUCH AMMO. WE'RE NOT GONNA WIN THIS HERE...WE JUST GOTTA HOLD 'EM HERE.
EL CAMINO, WATCH THE LEFT FLANK. YOU'RE GONNA GET HEAT THAT WAY, TOO, CHAVONNE. CHARGER, GET READY FOR SUPPORT.
YOU RIGHT, DEE. JUST LIKE YOU SAID.
HITS THE FAN
HOW IN THE FUCK DID THEY KNOW WE WERE COMING?
LAPD
CHARGERS GET THE MUTHAFUCKIN' JOB DONE!
BUDDA BUDDA

OKAY, GERALD. MAKE THE DELIVERY.
DAMNIT, DESTINY, HOW MANY TIMES DO I GOTTA TELL YOU, IT'S G-TRON.
'SCUSE ME... G-TRON.
POWNED
VROOOOOM
THANK GOD! SOME BACKUP! WE'RE OKAY, BOYS!
AND MOMS SAID VIDEOGAMES GOT NOTHING TO DO WIT' DA REAL WORLD...

BA-BOOM
FINISH THEM!
IT DIDN'T LAST LONG. THE ONES WHO DIDN'T FIGHT GAVE UP PRETTY QUICKLY.
PRISONERS OF WAR. OF *MY* WAR.
POLICE
THEY DIDN'T SEE THIS COMING. HOW COULD THEY? THEY HAVE NO IDEA WHAT TO DO WITH US.
WITH ME.

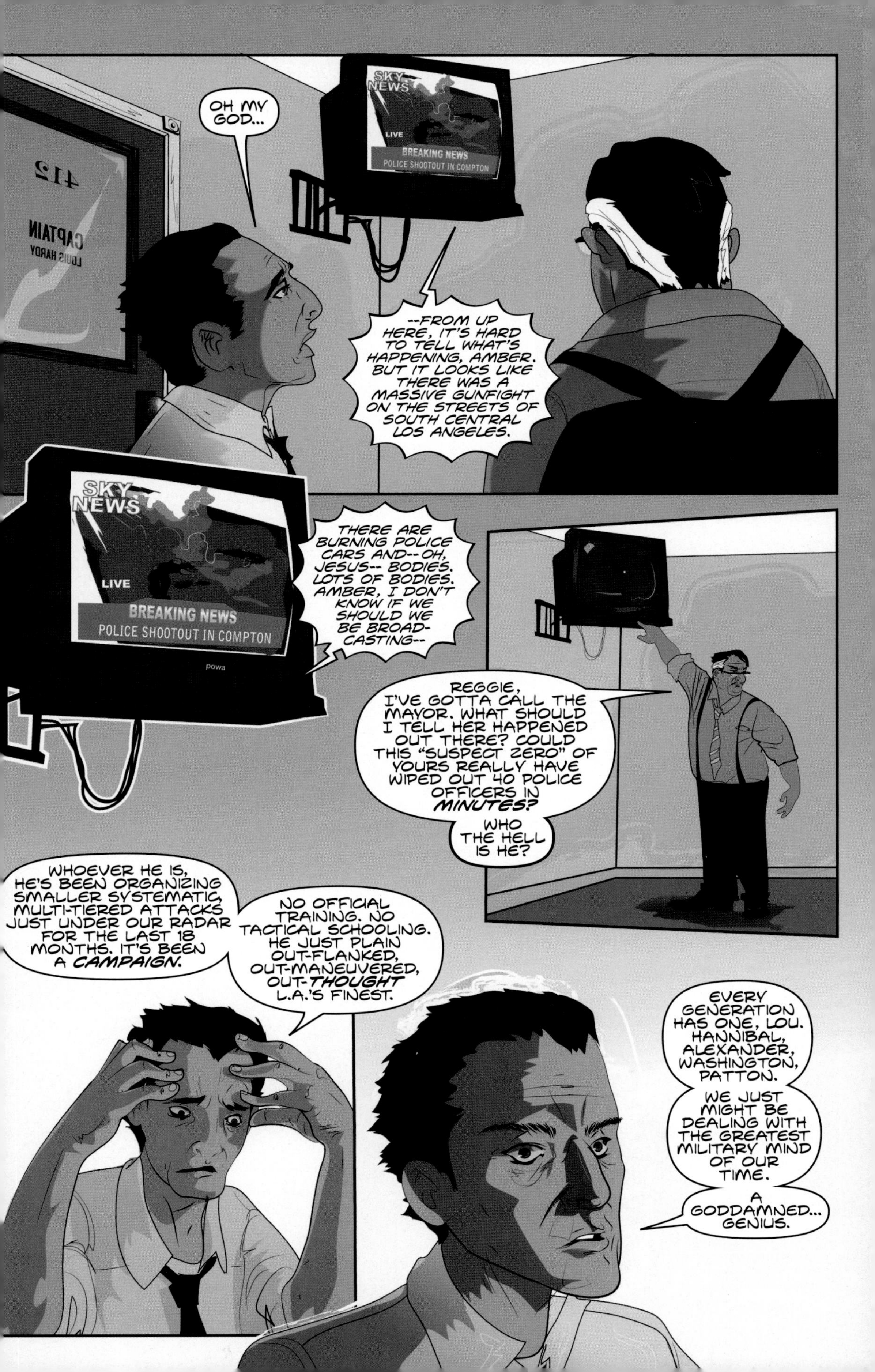
OH MY GOD...
SKY NEWS
LIVE
BREAKING NEWS
POLICE SHOOTOUT IN COMPTON
412
CAPTAIN
LOUIS HARDY
--FROM UP HERE, IT'S HARD TO TELL WHAT'S HAPPENING, AMBER. BUT IT LOOKS LIKE THERE WAS A MASSIVE GUNFIGHT ON THE STREETS OF SOUTH CENTRAL LOS ANGELES.
SKY NEWS
LIVE
BREAKING NEWS
POLICE SHOOTOUT IN COMPTON
THERE ARE BURNING POLICE CARS AND--OH, JESUS-- BODIES. LOTS OF BODIES. AMBER, I DON'T KNOW IF WE SHOULD WE BE BROAD-CASTING--
REGGIE, I'VE GOTTA CALL THE MAYOR. WHAT SHOULD I TELL HER HAPPENED OUT THERE? COULD THIS "SUSPECT ZERO" OF YOURS REALLY HAVE WIPED OUT 40 POLICE OFFICERS IN MINUTES?
WHO THE HELL IS HE?
WHOEVER HE IS, HE'S BEEN ORGANIZING SMALLER SYSTEMATIC, MULTI-TIERED ATTACKS JUST UNDER OUR RADAR FOR THE LAST 18 MONTHS. IT'S BEEN A CAMPAIGN.
NO OFFICIAL TRAINING. NO TACTICAL SCHOOLING. HE JUST PLAIN OUT-FLANKED, OUT-MANEUVERED, OUT-THOUGHT L.A.'S FINEST.
EVERY GENERATION HAS ONE, LOU. HANNIBAL, ALEXANDER, WASHINGTON, PATTON.
WE JUST MIGHT BE DEALING WITH THE GREATEST MILITARY MIND OF OUR TIME.
A GODDAMNED... GENIUS.

EL DORADO SQUAD: PICK UP THE WOUNDED AND TAKE 'EM TO MRS. TAYLOR'S HOUSE.
THE REST OF YOU, CLEAN YOUR GUNS AND CHECK YOUR AMMO.
BUT WE WON! WE JUS' KICKED DEY NARROW ASSES. SHIT'S *OVER!*
OVER? DAMNIT, FOOL.
WE JUST GETTIN' STARTED.

CHAPTER ONE

Brigadier General NAME REDACTED
fter more than a year of gang warfare at an all time ow, violence has erupted on the streets of Los Angeles. But this time it is different.
Destiny Ajaye, a 17-year-old resident of a six-block radius of South Central known as "Crossroads" has emerged from the shadows as the Commander-in-Chief of the recently unified gang populous. This petite, powerful, and brilliant young woman has somehow managed to unite all of the city's disparate factions into one army focused on one common enemy: the Los Angeles Police Department.
Saratoga County
Juvenile Correctional Facility
The "message" Destiny sends to the Police falls on deaf ears with the exception of Det. Reginald Grey. A cop by definition, an analyst by nature, Grey has spent the better part of a decade nurturing a theory to which only he subscribes. He hypothesizes that one enigmatic individual has been pulling the strings of the LA gangs to serve "his" bidding and build towards one possible outcome. War.
101 NORTH
Los Angeles
DETECTIVE REGINALD GREY
He calls this person "Suspect Zero" and when the faceless, sexless description of Destiny crosses his desk, Grey knows his "man" has finally made his move.
S.W.A.T
With an unexplainable, God-given talent for military strategy, Destiny uses her tactical genius to lead her newly trained army of gangbangers to a small victory over the 40 unsuspecting police officers sent in to investigate a cop killing.
While chaos takes hold at Police Headquarters, Destiny and her men lick their wounds and prepare for the coming onslaught...
Suspect Zero
FROM: Agent NAME REDACTED

Written by: Marc Bernardin & Adam Freeman   Art by: Afua Richardson

Letters by: Troy Peteri

RESPECT YOUR WEAPON, JAMAL. LAST THING YOU NEED IS SOME DIRTY SHIT BLOWIN' UP IN YOUR FACE.
DESTINY, WHAT'S THE PLAN? WHAT WE DOIN' JUST SITTIN' 'ROUND?
WHILE WE HERE ON OUR SSES THE COPS ARE GETTIN' THEIR SHIT TOGETHER.
NO ONE IS JUST SITTIN' 'ROUND. THIS IS A MARATHON, NOT A SPRINT. I NEED EVERYONE FRESH AND FROSTY. THIS MIGHT BE THE ONLY BREATH THEY HAVE FOR A WHILE.
THEY GONNA COME BACK HARD. WHO KNOWS WHAT THE PO-PO GOT PLANNED.
I DO.

GREY! GODDAMN IT-- GREY!
S.W.A.T
WHETHER THIS "SUSPECT ZERO" THEORY OF YOURS IS LEGIT OR NOT, YOU CAN'T GO INTO THE KILL ZONE. YOU BARELY EVEN QUALIFIED ON YOUR WEAPON.
I NEED YOU TO USE THAT BIG BRAIN WHERE IT CAN DO SOME GOOD.
WHAT DO YOU THINK I'M DOING? YOU'RE NOT GONNA WIN THIS--NO ONE'S GONNA WIN THIS--UNLESS WE KNOW EXACTLY WHAT AND WHO WE'RE DEALING WITH.
I HAVE SPENT THE SHITTIER PART OF THE LAST FIVE YEARS BUILDING A CASE ON THIS GUY.
WE NEED INFORMATION. WHO'S GONNA GET IT FOR US THESE GUYS?
LET ME DO WHAT I DO, LOU.
PLEASE.

IF YOU'VE GOTTA GO, GO HEAVY. RIDE IN WITH SWAT, AND BRING ME BACK SOMETHING I CAN USE.
THANKS, CAP.
LOS ANGELES
S.W.A.T.
SPECIAL WEAPONS AND TACTICAL
DON'T LET THIS ONE DO ANYTHING STUPID, SERGEANT.
STUPID HAPPENS, SIR. BUT HE WON'T GET HOLEY.
THEM CASUALTY NUMBERS ARE BULLSHIT, RIGHT? THEY GOTTA BE.
I BETCHA THE HEAD BANGER IN CHARGE IS A VET, MAN. DESERT STORM OR SOME SHIT. OFF HIS FUCKING NUT.
DON'T MATTER WHO HE IS, MAN. HE'S GOING DOWN. HARD.
BRAVADO ACCOMPLISHES ONE OF TWO GOALS: PUMPS UP THE WEAK OR SHOWS THE FEAR OF THE STRONG.
FOR THEIR SAKE I HOPE MY "SUSPECT ZERO" THEORY IS WRONG. IF NOT, THEY'RE ALL DEAD.

1993. LOS ANGELES.
"MY 'SUSPECT ZERO' PROBABLY GREW UP AROUND THE SAME NEIGHBORHOOD HE'S BLASTING TO THE GROUND.
"I DOUBT HE WAS THE KIND OF KID THAT PULLED WINGS OFF FLIES, BUT THERE WOULD'VE BEEN SIGNS OF AGGRESSION AT AN EARLY AGE.
!!!
!!!
1996.
"HE WAS PROBABLY A LONER...TOO SMART TO FIT IN.
LES' GET OUT OF HERE, MAN. WE AIN'T NEVER GONNA FIND HER.
I HATE PLAYING HIDE AND SEEK WIF THAT GIRL.
"BUT THERE WOULD NEED TO BE SOME KIND OF INCITING EVENT.
"A DEFINING MOMENT..."
POLICE
MOMMY?
"THE SPARK THAT IGNITES THE FLAME."

"FROM THERE, ALL THE DATA POINTS TO THE SYSTEM SINKING ITS CLAWS IN HIM.
POLICE LINE DO
POLICE LINE
POLICE LINE
425 SOCIAL SERVICES
NAH, MAN, I CAN TALK.
SAYS YOU! I BET THE UNDER. FUCKING RAIDERS. YEAH, TOMORROW SOUNDS GOOD...
"IN WELL-ADJUSTED HOMES IT IS COMMONPLACE FOR A CHILD TO DO ANYTHING FOR ATTENTION. ANYTHING TO STAND OUT--

"BUT FOR A PERSON THIS GIFTED, IN AN ENVIRONMENT WHERE DIFFERENT GETS YOU KILLED...
"...THE STREET-WISE PERSON WILL DO ANYTHING TO KEEP FROM GETTING NOTICED."
Which of the following countries was NOT an Axis Power:
a) Germany
b) Japan
c) Italy
d) Portugal

104
I BEEN TRYING TO BEAT THIS GAME FO' WEEKS, AND IT JUS KEEP ON KICKING MY ASS.
ROOM 104 COMPUTER LAB
WHAT IS IT, GERALD?
CHESS. LIKE CHECKERS BUT WITH A LOT MORE SHIT GOING ON.
"BUT SUSPECT ZERO COULDN'T LIVE AN ENTIRELY SOLITARY LIFE.
HOW DO EVERYTHING MOVE?
THESE LITTLE GUYS MOVE ONE SQUARE AT A TIME, UNLESS THEY'RE ATTACKING, THEN THEY GO DIAGONAL. THE DUDES WITH THE BIG HATS ALWAYS GO DIAGONAL.
THE HORSES MOVE IN "L"S. AND THE CASTLES GO UP, DOWN, AND ACROSS. THE KING IS THE PUNK-ASS-BITCH OF THE WHOLE GAME, BUT HE'S THE TARGET.
"HE'D FIND ONE OR TWO PEOPLE HE COULD BE HIMSELF WITH. PEOPLE HE COULD TRUST."
THE STRONGEST PIECE ON THE BOARD?
THE QUEEN.
I THINK... I THINK I LIKE THIS GAME.

WE STILL WIRED, GERALD?
LIKE I TOL' DEE--I FIXED EVERYTHING...
AND IT'S G-TRON. READ MY LIPS, G-TRON. DAMN.
EXT TIME, THEY'LL AVE AIR SUPPORT. HELICOPTERS.
SURPRISED DEY DIDN'T HAVE THEM EARLIER.
THEY UNDER-ESTIMATED US. THEY WON'T DO THAT AGAIN.
PWNED!
DID YOU HIT T BEVERLY HILLS TOY ORE? AND THAT DUDE IN K-TOWN?
GOT EVERYTHING ON THE LIST. BUT I'M NOT SURE HOW--
--AHHH. I GOT YOU. OKAY, I'LL GET TO WORK.

HOW LONG DO YOU THINK WE GOT?
IF THEY WERE SMART, THEY'D WAIT UNTIL 4 AM. WHEN THE HUMAN BODY IS AT IT'S LEAST ALERT.
BUT THEY WON'T BE SMART. THEY'LL BE ANGRY. AND ANGRY IS HOW WE WANT THEM.
BLDG 68
BLDG 66
DON'T FILL IT ALL THE WAY. WANT THE FUEL-AIR MIXTURE JUS' RIGHT.
I LIKE IT. EVERYONE MOVING WITH A PURPOSE. FOCUSED.
OCCUPY A MAN'S MIND AND IT KEEPS HIS ASS OUTTA TROUBLE. IT'S WHEN THEY JUST SITTIN' AROUND TALKING SMACK THAT THE SHIT GETS STIRRED UP.
WELL, D. DON'T KNOW HOW, DON'T CARE, BUT YOU DID IT, GIRL. CRIP, BLOOD, LATIN KINGS -- YOU GOT THEIR ASSES IN LINE.

"EVERY CULTURE, EVERY TRIBE, EVERY PACK-- EVERY GANG-- HAS AN ALPHA MALE.
"ALPHA'S RISE TO POWER CAN HAPPEN IN A NUMBER OF WAYS.
"IN A PACK OR PRIMITIVE TRIBE IT WILL MOST LIKELY BE THROUGH SHEER PHYSICAL PROWESS.
UT IN HIGHER-FUNCTIONING CIVILIZATIONS, THEY Y FIRST BECOME THE BETA MALE. A TRUSTED CONFIDANT OF THE CURRENT ALPHA MALE."
L-LAMONT, MAN... P-PLEASE...I JUST TOOK A TASTE, MAN. I WASN'T JACKIN' YOUR STUFF. P-PLEASE DON'T DO IT, DON'T POP ME...
DO IT.
BLAMM

"IF HE WAS JUST OUT TO PROVE HIS DICK WAS BIGGER, HE WOULD HAVE POPPED UP ON OUR RADAR A LONG TIME AGO.
MUMBLER
"NO, THIS ONE'S TOO SMART FOR THAT. STICK TO THE SHADOWS, LEARN THE GAME, THE PLAYERS...
"...AND THEN WHEN ALL THE RECON IS DONE. ALL THE DATA COLLECTED AND ANALYZED...
"...THE COUP D'ETAT."

TWO EARS AGO.
TRIADS, VICE LORDS, CULVER CITY BOYS, NORTENOS, ROLLIN' 30'S--
FOUR SEAS, MARA SALVATRUCHA, JOE BOYS--DAMN, LAMONT! YOU CALLED AND DEY CAME. DEY ALL HERE.
TONIGHT'S A NEW BEGINNING, BOYS.
STRAIGHT UP.
NO DISRESPECT, LAMONT.
ISS'ALL GOOD. IF WE ALL CLEAN, WE ALL SAFE. TONIGHT AIN'T ABOUT BLOOD.
YO! BRING IT IN! LISTEN UP!

THE OLD WAY IS OVER. DONE.
IF YOU DON'T AGREE... I CALL BULLSHIT-- 'CAUSE ALL YOU MUTHAFUCKERS ARE HERE.
OVER. DONE. YOU KNOW IT. I KNOW IT. BUT THAT AIN'T BAD. IT'S A GOOD THING. EVOLUTION AND SHIT.
WE ALL HURTIN.' BUSINESS AIN'T WHAT IT WAS.
'CAUSE YOU JACKED OUR SHIT IN CHINO LAST MONTH, PUTA!
AND NO ONE RESPECTS TERRITORIES ANY MORE!
RESPECT! YOU WANNA TALK RESPECT, YOU SLANTY-EYED MUTHAF--
YOU THINK YOU CAN POP MY BRO AND NOT TASTE BLOOD! I'LL FUCKIN' RIP YOUR FUCKIN' NUTS OUT THROUGH YOUR--
SHUT THE FUCK UP!
I'MA SAY IT AGAIN FOR YOU DEAF MUTHAFUCKERS.
SHUT. THE. FUCK. UP.

YOU KNOW WHAT I SEE?
I SEE DEAD MEN. THEY JUST DON'T KNOW IT YET.
LAMONT, MAN, YOU BEST TELL YOUR DIMEPIECE TO CLOSE HER FUCKIN' MOUTH OR--
KRAKK
UNGGH!
OH SHIT!
WHEN I SAY SO, SEND YOUR #1 MAN DOWN FRONT.
VICE LORDS. ROLLIN' 30'S. ROLLIN' 60'S. BIG CIRCLE GANG. FOUR SEAS. WO HOP TO. CLANTON 14. MARA 18. BLACK P. STONES...
YOU ALL KNOW ME. YOU KNOW WHO I ROLL WIT. DON'T MATTER NO MORE. HISTORY IS DEAD.
WE DON'T STAND TOGETHER, WE DIE. WE ALREADY DYIN'. FROM TODAY FORWARD-- ONE VOICE.
OH YEAH? AND LEMME GUESS WHO DAT VOICE IS. YOUR MAN LAMONT.

NO...
BLAMM
BLAMM
BLAMM
BLAMM
ME.

DESTINY...
DESTINY! THEY COMIN'.
COPY THAT. THANK YOU.
GOOD, GOOD. GET THAT STUFF OFF THE STREET. AIR SUPPORT WILL BE HERE SOON AND I DON'T WANT THEM SPOTTIN' NUTHIN'.
HUDDLE UP, PEOPLE. REMEMBER WHEN WE TALKED ABOUT "ECONOMY OF FORCE" AND "PEPPERPOTTING?" THIS HERE WILL BE YOUR FINAL EXAM...
POLICE

YO, GREY! YOU LOOK LIKE YOU'RE ABOUT TO TOSS YOUR GODDAMN COOKIES!
PUSHIN' ALL THOSE PENCILS HAS MADE YOU SOFT, REGINALD! THAT'S WHAT I THINK.
YOU KNOW WHAT I THINK?
I THINK YOU ALL ARE ABOUT TO HAVE YOUR ASSES HAN--
KABLOOOOOM
POLICE
LOS ANGELES SWAT POLICE
SERGEANT

CAMINOS: HIT 'EM WITH SOMETHING PRETTY.
FUCK! WE GOT INCOMING!
NEGATIVE. NEGATIVE. WE'RE NOT TAKING HITS BUT HOLD HERE-- IT'S FUCKING WITH OUR GUIDANCE AND I DON'T WANT US TAKING EACH OTHER DOWN.
PULL UP! PULL UP!
NOW, GERALD: HIT 'EM WITH SOMETHING HARD.
ARE THOSE REMOTE-CONTROL HELICOPTERS?
PULL UP!
WHA BOOOOM

KABLOOOM
BADOOOM
GREY!
GREY! FOLLOW ME! GREY! GET DOWN AND FOLLOW ME!
KRAK!

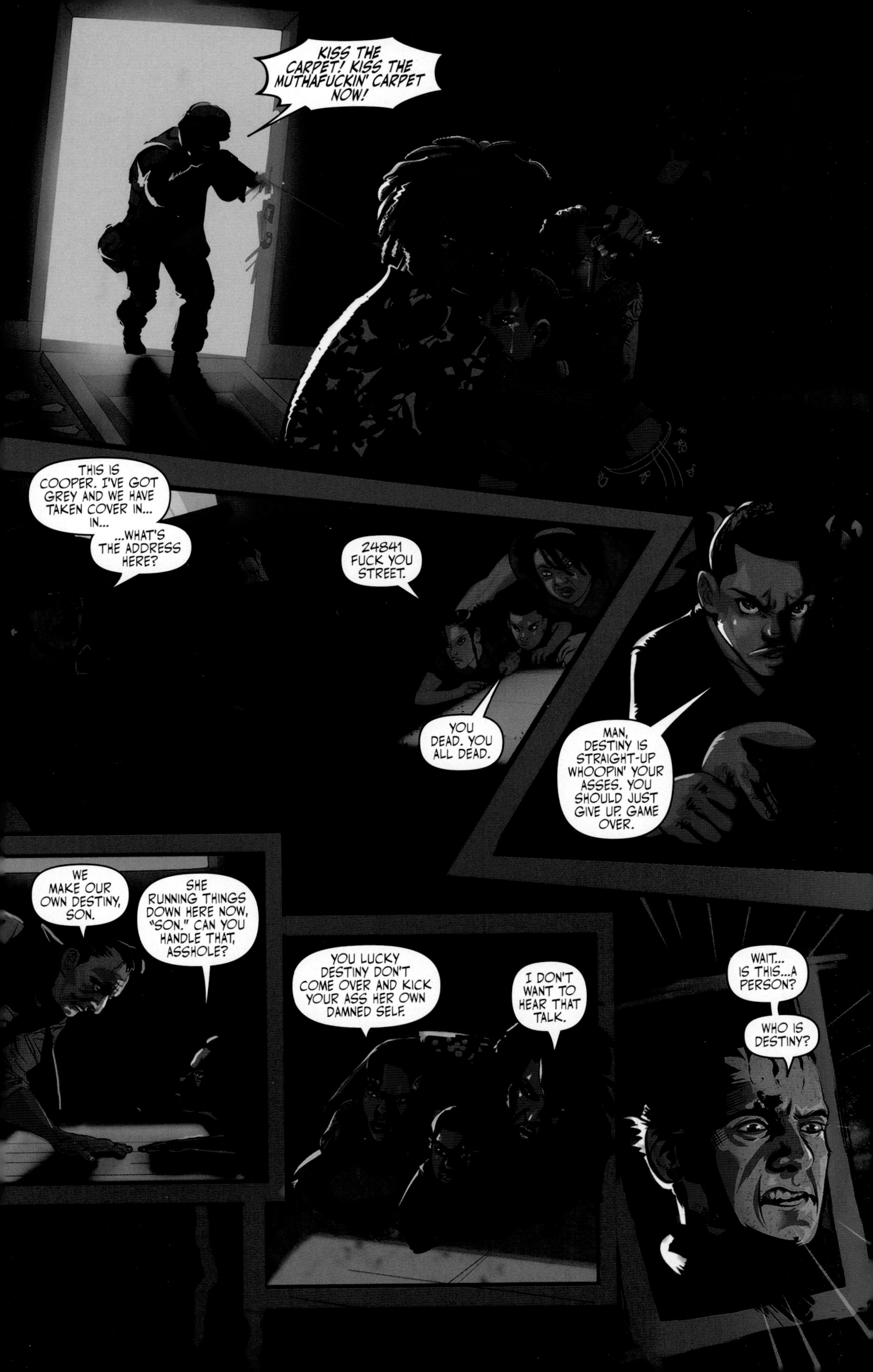
KISS THE CARPET! KISS THE MUTHAFUCKIN' CARPET NOW!
THIS IS COOPER. I'VE GOT GREY AND WE HAVE TAKEN COVER IN... IN...
...WHAT'S THE ADDRESS HERE?
24841 FUCK YOU STREET.
YOU DEAD. YOU ALL DEAD.
MAN, DESTINY IS STRAIGHT-UP WHOOPIN' YOUR ASSES. YOU SHOULD JUST GIVE UP. GAME OVER.
WE MAKE OUR OWN DESTINY, SON.
SHE RUNNING THINGS DOWN HERE NOW, "SON." CAN YOU HANDLE THAT, ASSHOLE?
YOU LUCKY DESTINY DON'T COME OVER AND KICK YOUR ASS HER OWN DAMNED SELF.
I DON'T WANT TO HEAR THAT TALK.
WAIT... IS THIS...A PERSON?
WHO IS DESTINY?

CHAPTER TWO

"SO WE HAVE NO IDEA WHAT'S GOING ON IN THERE?"
"NO CLUE WHO'S LIVING OR DYING?"
"THIS, PEOPLE, IS WHAT WE CALL UNACCEPTABLE."

THIS --WHAT ARE WE CALLING IT?--THIS "SOUTH CENTRAL SIEGE" HAS BEEN GOING ON FOR 12 HOURS NOW AND WHAT DO WE HAVE TO SHOW FOR IT.
NOTHING!
KLA NEWS 8
WELL, WE'VE BEEN RUNNING THAT "FACES OF THE HOOD" SERIES...YOU KNOW, THE MUG SHOTS OF PREVIOUSLY ARRESTED GANG-BANGERS.
AND HOW'S THAT DOING?
NOT GOOD.
PERFECT. THIS IS A NEWS CHANNEL AND WE DON'T HAVE ANY GODDAMNED NEWS!
WHERE'S OUR EYE IN THE FUCKING SKY? WE'RE CUTTING TO THAT SAME AERIAL FOOTAGE WE SHOT WHEN IT STARTED.
BUT, IZZY... SOMEONE'S SHOOTING DOWN POLICE HELICOPTERS. OUR GUYS WON'T--
WE PAY THEM FIVE TIMES WHAT COPS MAKE. YOU TELL THEM TO GET THEIR ASSES IN THE AIR.
HALF OF THEM FLEW IN IRAQ FOR FUCK'S SAKE, THEY CAN HANDLE THIS SHIT.

KLA NEWS 8
MISS CORTINA? I THINK I'VE GOT SOMETHING...
LEAVE IT TO THE FUCKING INTERN TO RAISE HIS HAND.
THIS POPPED UP ON A FEW STREAMING SITES A COUPLE OF HOURS AGO AND IT'S GOING VIRAL. I TRACKED IT BACK TO THE ORIGINAL IP ADDRESS.
IN SOUTH CENTRAL.
MY SON WAS KILLED BY THE MEN SENT TO SERVE AND PROTECT US. YES, HE SOLD DRUGS. HE DID WHATEVER HE HAD TO DO TO FEED HIS FAMILY.
WHEN HE DIDN'T HAVE ENOUGH TO GIVE THE POLICE THEIR CUT... GONE.
4:20 / 5:00
I ASK MY MOMS IF I WAS IN JAIL. SHE SAID, "WHY YOU SAY THAT?" I TOLD HER "CAUSE WE GOT ALL DEM BARS ON OUR WINDOWS AND DOORS."
SHE SAID, "IT AIN'T SUPPOSED TO BE THIS WAY." WHATEVER THAT MEANS.
ME TUBE
IF YOU WAS IN THE JUNGLE YOU'D DO WHAT YOU NEED TO SURVIVE, RIGHT? YOU'D KILL SHIT, YOU'D STEAL SHIT FROM ANOTHER TRIBE IF MEANT STARVING OR NOT.
WELL, WE IN THE JUNGLE, MOTHER-FUCKER.
2:40 / 5:00
ANYONE ELSE HAVE THIS YET?
NOT THAT I'VE SEEN, MA'AM.
SEND THE LINK TO GRAPHICS. HAVE 'EM RIP IT AND PREP FOR BROADCAST.
LET'S OWN THIS SHIT.

CHARGER 2, YOUR HEAD-CAM IS STATIC-Y. OKAY, GOOD.
THUNDERBIRD 1, WATCH YOUR LEFT.
EL DORADO SQUAD. GAS MASKS AT THE READY. THEY'RE GONNA COME WITH PEPPER GRENADES SOON.
CAVALIER, GET READY TO PUSH. AND MAKE IT LOOK LIKE WE WANT THAT STREET.
DEE, YOUR LITTLE HOME MOVIES IS STARTIN' TO RACK UP THE HITS.
LEMME KNOW WHEN THE NETWORKS GRAB IT.
IF WE ONLY FIGHT THE WAR ON THE STREET...WE LOSE.
PLATO
ARMED MADHOUSE
THE PEOPLE'S HISTORY OF THE UNITED STATES
CHOCOLATE RAI

DESTINY? SAY THAT AGAIN: WHAT ABOUT DESTINY?
I SAID SHE GONNA KICK YO ASS. ALL YO ASSES.
SHE? OKAY -- HOLD UP A SECOND...
HE DON'T KNOW WHAT HE SAYIN'. NEVER MIND HIM.
DO TOO!
SHE SAID SHUT YOUR PUNK MOUTH, CALVIN!
BOTH OF YOU... ENOUGH.
IS THAT WHO'S RUNNING THINGS? THIS DESTINY? WHO IS SHE?
BOY, WHEN THIS IS ALL OVER... I'M GONNA SMACK THE BLACK RIGHT OFFA YOU.

WE CAN'T STAY HERE.
WHAT MAKES YOU THINK WE LEAVIN'?
OKAY, WE'RE GOING TO MOVE. CAN YOU ALL RUN? NO ONE HURT?
AND RIGHT NOW, ONLY ON KLA NEWS 8, A LOOK AT THE FAMILIES CAUGHT IN THE CROSSFIRE OF WHAT HAS NOW BEEN DUBBED THE "SOUTH CENTRAL SIEGE."
TURN THAT UP!
LIVE
SOUTH CENTRAL SEIGE
FAMILIES CAUGHT IN THE CROSSFIRE
BREAKING NEWS
KLA NEWS 8
CITY UNDER SEIGE
I'VE SEEN ALL THE RIOTS: WATTS, KING -- WELL, BOTH KINGS. I'VE BEEN HIT WITH THE HOSES, TOO.
LIVE
BUT THIS HERE... THIS IS DIFFERENT. WE'RE NOT PROTESTING. WE'RE FIGHTING FOR OUR LIVES HERE. FOLKS GOTS TO KNOW...
KLA NEWS 8
FAMILIES CAUGHT IN THE CROSSFIRE
WE ARE IN WAY OVER OUR HEADS.

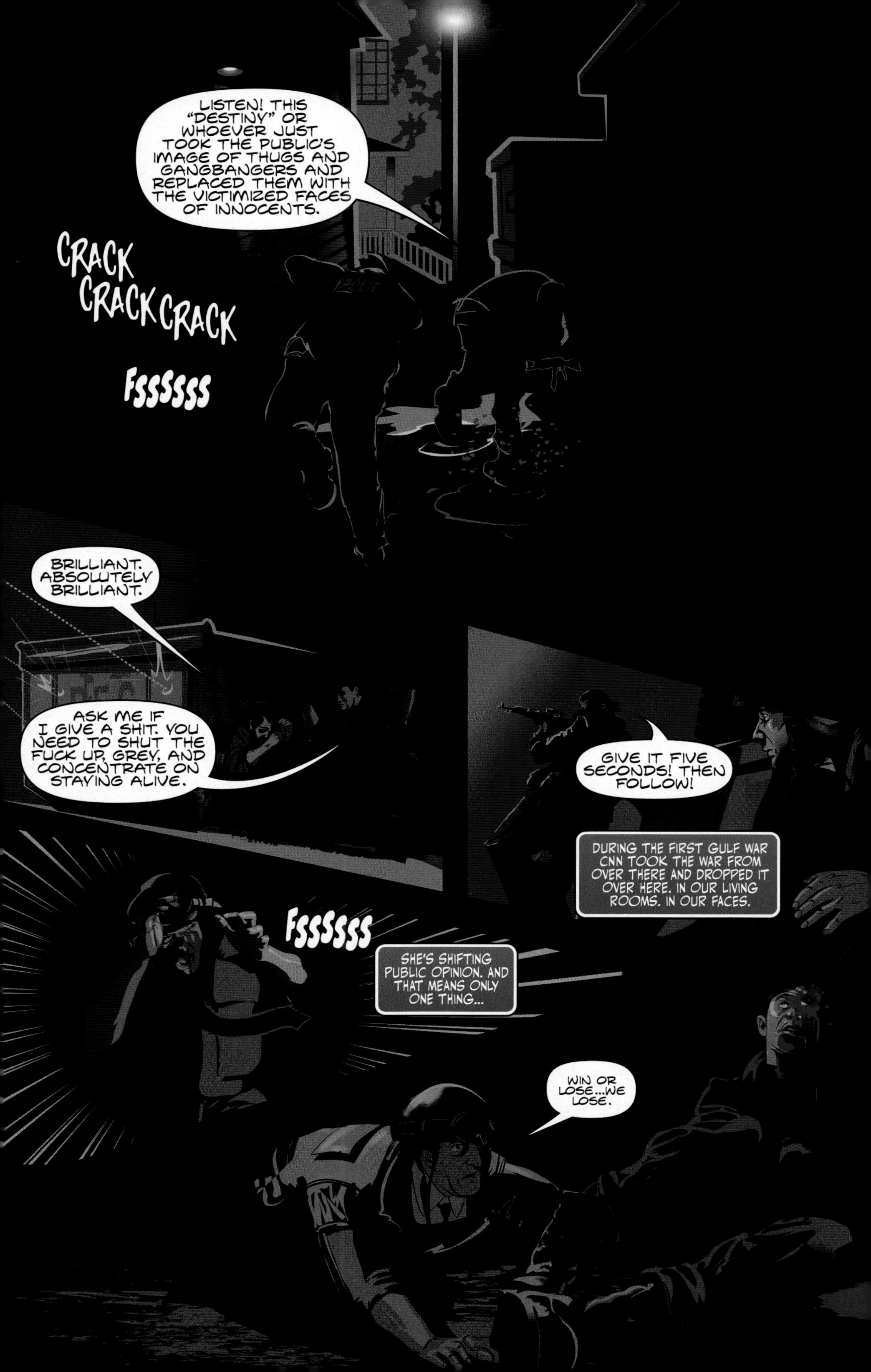

LISTEN! THIS "DESTINY" OR WHOEVER JUST TOOK THE PUBLIC'S IMAGE OF THUGS AND GANGBANGERS AND REPLACED THEM WITH THE VICTIMIZED FACES OF INNOCENTS.
CRACK
CRACK CRACK
FSSSSSS
BRILLIANT. ABSOLUTELY BRILLIANT.
ASK ME IF I GIVE A SHIT. YOU NEED TO SHUT THE FUCK UP, GREY, AND CONCENTRATE ON STAYING ALIVE.
GIVE IT FIVE SECONDS! THEN FOLLOW!
DURING THE FIRST GULF WAR CNN TOOK THE WAR FROM OVER THERE AND DROPPED IT OVER HERE. IN OUR LIVING ROOMS. IN OUR FACES.
FSSSSSS
SHE'S SHIFTING PUBLIC OPINION. AND THAT MEANS ONLY ONE THING...
WIN OR LOSE...WE LOSE.

YOU GOTTA LOVE THOSE INTERNETS.

PACK THOSE RAGS TIGHT, YOU HEAR? AND IF YOU SO MUCH AS GOT TO SNEEZE YOU GO OUTSIDE. RESPECT THAT SHIT.

DESTINY! YO, DEE! THEY NEED YOU UP TOP.

IS THAT THE MARINES?

NAH...WHEN THEY COME HEAVY, IT WON'T BE THE MARINES. IT'LL BE THE NATIONAL GUARD.

BUT WE AIN'T THERE YET. SO FAR, WE DONE BUT TOOK OUT A SWAT VAN AND FIVE COP CARS. NINETEEN MEN.

THEY CAN LOSE THAT MANY ON THREE OR FOUR FUCKED DRUG BUSTS. IT'S STILL IN LAPD'S HANDS.

THASS GOOD, THO, RIGHT? JUST THE COPS?

WE COULDA KILLED COPS ANY DAMNED DAY. I'M IN IT FOR THE BRASS MOTHERFUCKING RING.

WELL, DAMN IT, YOU FIND A WAY! WE ARE GONNA GET ONE LAST SHOT AT THIS, SERGEANT BROD. THEN IT GOES FEDERAL.
SWAT NEEDS TO TAKE BACK THAT REAL ESTATE, OR I TAKE THIS OUT OF YOUR HANDS... BECAUSE IT'LL GET TAKEN OUT OF MINE.
I CAN PUSH ALL I WANT, MR. MAYOR. THEY'RE NOT SITTING ON THEIR HANDS OUT THERE... THEY'RE GETTING KILLED.
Captain James Hardy
LAPD SWAT IS SUPPOSED TO BE THE BEST AT WHAT THEY DO. AND THEY ARE GETTING THEIR ASSES HANDED TO THEM.
AND SO AM I. HAVE YOU SEEN THOSE ONLINE VIDEOS THE NEWS HAVE BEEN AIRING? KIDS, GRANDPARENTS, FAMILIES...WE ARE LOSING THE MORAL HIGH GROUND.
AND THAT'LL KILL YOU JUST AS DEAD AS LOSING THE LITERAL HIGH GROUND, JUST SLOWER.

...AND NOW, ANOTHER KLA EXCLUSIVE. WE HAVE NOW LEARNED, FROM RELIABLE SOURCES, THAT SIX OF THE SLAIN OFFICERS WERE OTHERWISE KNOWN AS "THE BLUE CIRCLE," A RING OF CORRUPT COPS KNOWN FOR EXTORTION AND DRUG DEALING AMONG OTHER OFFENSES...
POLICE CORRUPTION?
LAPD SCANDAL
EXPOSED
KLA NEWS 8
weather forcast:SOUTH GATE, CALIFORNIA (PWS)
...THIS IS NO DIFFERENT. CRIMINALS PREYING ON L.A.'S FINEST. KILLING THE SAME BRAVE MEN AND WOMEN THAT HAVE TAKEN AN OATH TO PROTECT THEM.
DONALD, I BEG TO DIFFER. WHAT WE HAVE HERE IS A PEOPLE, NOT UNLIKE THIS COUNTRY'S FOREFATHERS, OPPRESSED BY THE RULE OF TYRANNICAL MEN. WHY WAS IT OKAY FOR THE WHITE SETTLERS TO RISE AGAINST THE BRITISH BUT NOT OKAY FOR TODAY'S MINORITIES TO DO THE SAME?
LIVE
GOOD DAY LA HEAD TO HEAD
CITIZENS WAGE WAR ON LAPD
10:45 78°
SHART
Y'ALL LOOKED AT US LIKE WE WUZ CRAZY! WE DONE BETTER THAN THAT NOSTRODUMBASS FELLA. WE SAID THEY WAS ANIMALS AND THEY WOULD ESCAPE THE ZOO AND WE WAS RIGHT. CASE CLOSED.
TOP LINE
FALLEN HEROES OR SLAIN VILLAINS? THAT QUESTION AND MORE ANSWERED TONIGHT AT 11.
NEWS AT ELEVEN
FONY
POWER
...AND WE ARE NOW HEARING THAT LEADERS OF THE AFRICAN AMERICAN COMMUNITY, INCLUDING THE REV. AL SHARPTON AND JIM BROWN, ARE MEETING BEHIND CLOSED DOORS TO DISCUSS THE BEST PLAN OF ACTION...

GOTTA GET THE HELL BACK...
HEY, DEE! WE GOT A RUNNER. WAN' ME TO HAVE HIM POPPED?
BOUNCE IT UP TO THE BIG SCREEN, GERALD.
CAM 03 19:25
NAH...LOOK AT HIM. MOTHERFUCKER LOOKS LIKE HE SHIT HIMSELF SCARED. NO WEAPON. LET 'IM GO.
BUT WE GOT ANOTHER PROBLEM.

THEY CUT THE POWER. WHICH MEANS THEY'RE COMING. ***NOW.*** GERALD, GENERATORS.
YOU'RE THE EYES AND EARS NOW, GERALD. YOU KEEP US STRAIGHT.
WHEN THEY JAM THE WALKIES, SWITCH US OVER.
PATCH ME IN TO EVERYONE.
NO SIGNAL

Y'ALL KNOW WHAT TO DO. WE PUSH. MAKE THEM PAY FOR EVERY GODDAMN INCH WE GIVE THEM. THERE'S A WHOLE LOT OF US NIGGERS, CHINKS, AND SPICS DEY GONNA HAVE TO GET THROUGH.
SHOW THEM WHO WE ARE!

IT'S HAPPENING!
TAKE US DOWN! WE GOTTA GET DOWN THERE!
LA NEWS 8

FUCK THAT! I SHOULDN'T EVEN BE THIS CLOSE. IF THOSE ANIMALS DON'T SHOOT US DOWN, LAPD WILL.
GROW A PAIR! THEN SET ME AND LANCE DOWN ON A ROOF SOMEWHERE.
I'M WITH HIM, IZZY. THIS IS FUCKING CRAZY. I SAY WE BANG OFF SOME B-ROLL SHOTS FROM UP HERE AND PULL BACK.
JESUS CHRIST! WHY IS IT THAT I'VE GOT THE BIGGEST BALLS ON THIS FUCKING HELICOPTER?
SPLIT THE DIFFERENCE. TAKE ME DOWN TO 60 FEET AND THEN YOU CAN BUG OUT OF HERE.
WE GOT THE 21-U UP HERE? BETTER BE LOADED AND CHARGED!
KLA NEWS 8
ALWAYS.
HAND ME THAT GARBAGE BAG.
WHY?

FUCK! ME!
PPPPLLAAAASHHHH
SHE'S FUCKING NUTS.
COOP, GET US OUT OF HERE.
Fly
Emirate

POLICE
OH FU--
EASY. LET'S SEE THOSE HANDS.
YOU DON'T LOOK LIKE THIS IS YOUR NATURAL HABITAT.
I-I'M ON THE J-JOB.
GET HIM BACK TO THE TRUCK, TANNER. WALK 'EM BACK YOURSELF. ONE BLOCK SOUTH.
I'M A DETECTIVE--
THIS ISN'T A CRIME SCENE ANYMORE. IT'S A WAR ZONE AND YOU'RE GONNA GET YOURSELF, OR WORSE, ONE OF US KILLED.
YES, SIR. MOVE TO SUPPORT THE COLUMN ON APPROACH PATH DELTA. ON OUR WAY.

HIT 'EM!
FUCK YO' COUCH
FWIP
THWIP
OH, GOD...

PING
ZING
POLICE
CRACK
UNNGGH!
ALL UNITS...FALL BACK.
WHAT SHE JUST SAY?
REPEAT. FALL BACK. SINGLE COLUMN.
BUT WE CAN TAKE 'EM. WE GOT THIS.
CRACK
B-B-BANG
THEY'RE FALLING BACK! WHAT SHOULD WE DO?
UNGGH!
ARGHH!
POLICE
POLICE
DAMN IT, SON! ADVANCE!

EVERYBODY... PUSH!
LOS ANGELES SWAT POLICE
SERGEANT
GERALD, WE STILL GREEN?
YEAH, DESTINY. ONE OR TWO GOT HIT IN THE CROSSFIRE, BUT ENOUGH'LL GO TO SPARK 'EM ALL.
GOOD.
WHAT'S HAPPENING?
WE'RE ADVANCING. EVERY INCH IS COSTING US, BUT WE'RE GAINING GROUND.
LOS ANGELES SPECIAL WEAPONS AND TACTICAL
MOBILE COMMAND
911
POLICE
LAPD
SERGEANT
GOOD... GOOD.
WAIT... YOU'RE ADVANCING ON EVERY FRONT?
GET YOUR MEN OUT OF THERE. NOW!

GERALD! BLOW IT!
KRA-BO
BLIP... BLIP...

OH MY GOD...
WE'RE DONE HERE. I'M CALLING IN THE FUCKING NATIONAL GUARD.
PWR REC

WELL DONE. NOW WE GOTTA--
WHAT. THE. FUCK.

IT WAS A TACTICAL MOVE DESIGNED TO--

FUCK "TACTICAL," DEE.
THERE IS A DIFFERENCE BETWEEN SOLDIERS...
RUN N TELL THAT

24
...AND PAWNS.

CHAPTER THREE

EVERYTHING STARTS SOMEWHERE.
YOU TRACE ANYTHING BACK FAR ENOUGH, YOU'LL FIND A CHOICE.
BAD GUY HIGH
SOMEONE WHO DECIDED TO ACT. OR NOT TO ACT.
BUT THE WORLD NEVER CHANGED FOR ANYONE BECAUSE SHE SAT ON HER ASS.
YOU GOTTA TAKE YOUR SHOT.

BANG
A GUN IS JUST A TOOL.
BLAM
BANG
fssssssss
LIKE A LEVER. OR PIPE WRENCH.
AIN'T NOTHING BUT A MEANS TO GET A JOB DONE
BANG-PTING

BURGER HUT
BURGER HUT
SO, YOU NOW WHAT OU GOTTA O, RIGHT?

YEAH. I KNOW.

YOU WANNA ROLL WIT US, YOU WANNA BE A CRIP -- WIT ALL THAT MOTHERFUCKING IMPLIES -- YOU GOTTA BLEED A FOOL.

DON' COME BACK IF YOU DON' SMELL LIKE PISTOL. AND DON' BITCH OUT NEITHER!

BURGER HUT. CAN I HELP YOU?
DRINK SM .99 MED 1.50 LG 2.00
FRIES / SALAD / RICH N BEANS
CHILLI / BAKED TATER / CORN
SM .99 MED 1.15 LG 1.50
WHEN FACED WITH A FORK IN THE ROAD...
BANG
BANG
COULD I CHOOSE TO DO WHAT HAD TO BE DONE?
YEAH. I COULD.
I COULD KILL A MAN AND BE OKAY WITH IT. BUSINESS. NOT PERSONAL. A MEANS TO AN END.
AND THAT END...
Bloodz

HERE.
HAT THE CK, DEE? WE WAS UPPOSED WIN THIS SHIT.
WE WAS GONNA "RAIN DOWN DESTRUCTION ON THESE MOTHERFUCKERS." THAT'S WHAT YOU SAID. AIN'T SAID NOTHING ABOUT US GETTIN' KILLED, TOO.
YEAH.
WE DONE HAD JUST ABOUT ENOUGH.
RUN N TELL THAT

WE ARE FIGHTING A WAR. WHAT PART OF "WAR" MADE YOU THINK NO ONE WAS GONNA GET HURT?
I TOLD YOU APPARENTLY IGNORANT BITCHES THAT WE WERE GONNA CHANGE OUR WORLD.
AND CHANGE ALWAYS COMES WITH BLOOD.
YEAH, WE LOST SOME PEOPLE. AND WE'RE GONNA LOSE MORE.
MY JOB ISN'T TO KEEP YOU PUSSIES FROM DYING, IT'S TO MAKE SURE THOSE DEATHS WEREN'T WASTED. THAT THEY COUNT FOR SOMETHING.
YOU WANNA GET POPPED IN A BODEGA? OR ON THE FIELD OF BATTLE?
ANY ONE OF YOU THINK YOU CAN STEP UP AN' RUN THIS SHIT, COME ON, THEN.
SURE IS QUIET.
IT'S A NEW DAY. A DAY THAT WON'T SEE ANY POLICE CRUISERS ON THE STREET. WON'T SEE ANY DRIVE-BYS.
THE COPS ARE GONNA KEEP THEIR DISTANCE FOR A BIT. TRY AND FIGURE OUT HOW THEY FUCKED UP SO BAD.
I'MA GO ENJOY MYSELF. Y'ALL DO WHAT YOU WANT.

SO, WHAT, WE JUST STAND HERE?
DON'T FIRE UNLESS FIRED UPON. THAT'S THE WORD, THAT'S WHAT WE DO.
WE JUST SUPPOSED TO *AIM* THEM TO DEATH?
WE SUPPOSED TO KEEP THEM OUT. THEY AIN'T TRYING TO GET IN, THEY COOL. THEY HOP THE FENCE, THEY GET DROPPED.
CAMERAS ARE CLEAR, DEE. ALL POINTS ARE REPORTING A LACK OF ACTION.
IT'S QUIET. I DON'T EVER REMEMBER IT BEING THIS QUIET.

IS IT OVER?
NO. NOT YET. BUT WE'VE GOT A LITTLE BREAK, IF YOU WANNA WALK A BIT.

CLIK
BOOM THUM THUM BOOM THUM THUM BOOM THUM THUM

ROTATE SHIFTS ON AND OFF THE FRONT LINES. IF YOU AIN'T ON, HAVE FUN. Y'ALL HAVE EARNED IT.
Track 01 Dr.Foo
BOOMTHUMTHUMBOOMTHUMTHUMBOOMTHU

BOOMTHUMTHUMBOOMTHUMTHUMBOOMTHU

HOW OLD ARE YOU, KID?
TODAY? OLD ENOUGH.
YEAH. ME, TOO.

KIDS ARE RESILIENT. AMAZES ME HOW THEY CAN JUST...LET GO.
I DON'T KNOW WHETHER THAT SHOULD BE HEARTENING OR DEPRESSING.
Morningside
BOOM THUM THUM BOOM THUM THUM BOOM THUM TH
THE GUNFIRE HAS BECOME WHITE NOISE TO THEM.
THIS IS THE DREAM, CHAVONNE. THIS IS WHAT IT'S FOR.
EVEN IF IT CAN'T LAST.
NOW AIN'T O TIME FOR A FUCKING PARTY...
ACTUALLY, SOLDIERS HAVE DONE AS MUCH SINCE THE BRONZE AGE. RAISE A JOYFUL NOISE SO EVEN THE GODS CAN HEAR. LET THEM KNOW SOULS FULL OF LIFE ARE ON THE WAY.
WHATEVER, BRANIAC. FUCKED UP IS WHAT IT IS.

THEY DESERVE THEIR PARTY. THEY WON.
DESTINY HAS ROCKED ONE OF AMERICA'S FINEST POLICE FORCES -- A SMALL ARMY -- ON ITS HEELS. AND SHE'S DONE IT MORE THAN ONCE.
Bottega Louie
POLICE
WE COULD ALWAYS WAIT THEM OUT. AT SOME POINT, THEY'LL RUN OUT OF FOOD. WE ALREADY SHUT OFF THE WATER.
WE'VE GOT TO DO MORE THAN "BE PATIENT." IS MY OFFICIAL STATEMENT READY?
YOU'RE ALIVE, THEN. GOOD. DID YOU GET ALL THE DATA YOU NEEDED?
YOU'RE GETTING YOUR ASS KICKED BY A TEENAGED GIRL NAMED DESTINY.
FUCK ME.

BURGER HUT
BURGER HUT
SO, YOU NOW WHAT OU GOTTA O, RIGHT?

YEAH. I KNOW.

YOU WANNA ROLL WIT US, YOU WANNA BE A CRIP -- WIT ALL THAT MOTHERFUCKING IMPLIES -- YOU GOTTA BLEED A FOOL.

DON' COME BACK IF YOU DON' SMELL LIKE PISTOL. AND DON' BITCH OUT NEITHER!

BURGER HUT. CAN I HELP YOU?
WHEN FACED WITH A FORK IN THE ROAD...
BANG BANG BAN
COULD I CHOOSE TO DO WHAT HAD TO BE DONE?
YEAH. I COULD.
I COULD KILL A MAN AND BE OKAY WITH IT. BUSINESS. NOT PERSONAL. A MEANS TO AN END.
AND THAT END...

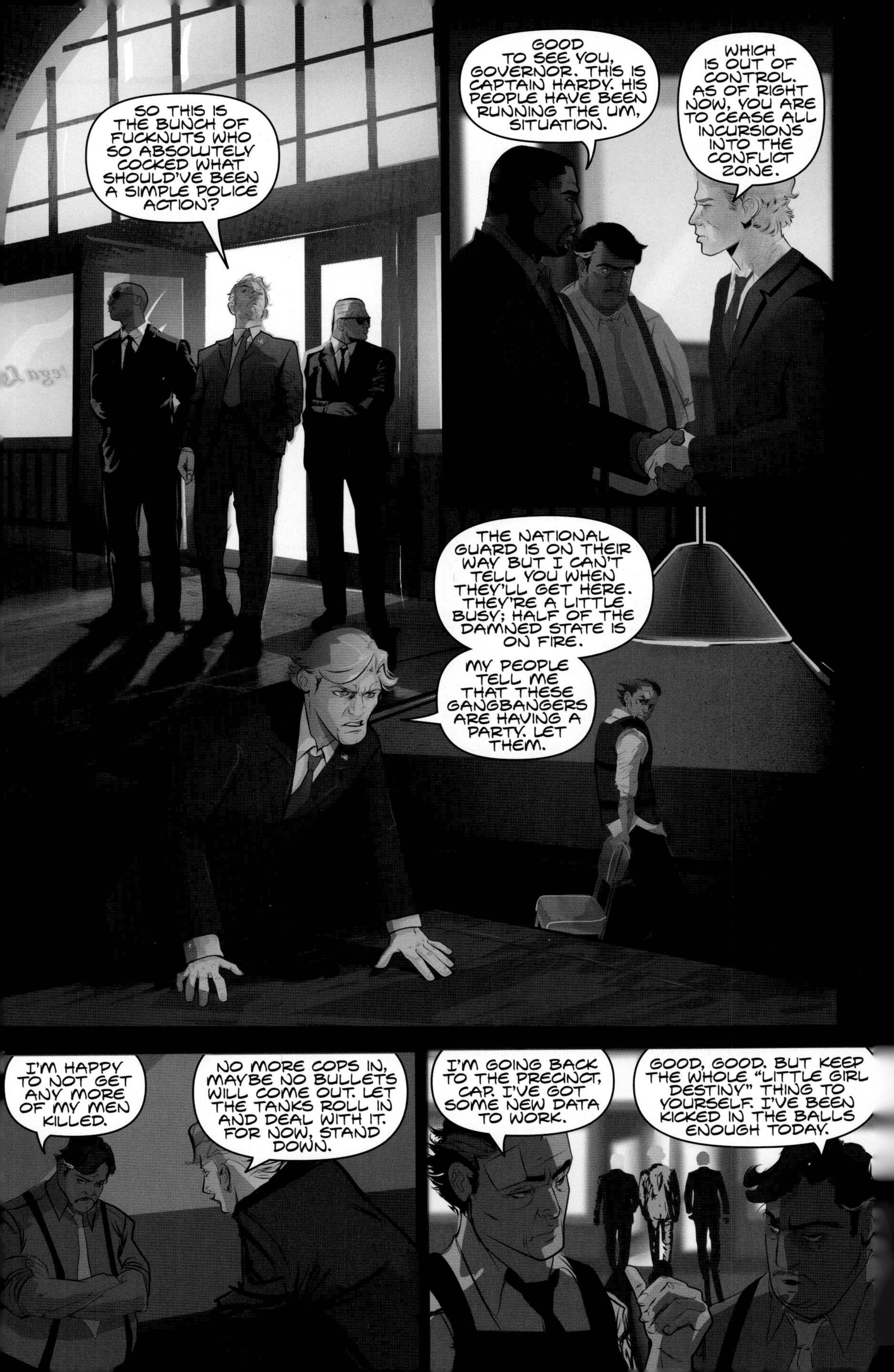
SO THIS IS THE BUNCH OF FUCKNUTS WHO SO ABSOLUTELY COCKED WHAT SHOULD'VE BEEN A SIMPLE POLICE ACTION?
GOOD TO SEE YOU, GOVERNOR. THIS IS CAPTAIN HARDY. HIS PEOPLE HAVE BEEN RUNNING THE UM, SITUATION.
WHICH IS OUT OF CONTROL. AS OF RIGHT NOW, YOU ARE TO CEASE ALL INCURSIONS INTO THE CONFLICT ZONE.
THE NATIONAL GUARD IS ON THEIR WAY BUT I CAN'T TELL YOU WHEN THEY'LL GET HERE. THEY'RE A LITTLE BUSY; HALF OF THE DAMNED STATE IS ON FIRE.
MY PEOPLE TELL ME THAT THESE GANGBANGERS ARE HAVING A PARTY. LET THEM.
I'M HAPPY TO NOT GET ANY MORE OF MY MEN KILLED.
NO MORE COPS IN, MAYBE NO BULLETS WILL COME OUT. LET THE TANKS ROLL IN AND DEAL WITH IT. FOR NOW, STAND DOWN.
I'M GOING BACK TO THE PRECINCT, CAP. I'VE GOT SOME NEW DATA TO WORK.
GOOD, GOOD. BUT KEEP THE WHOLE "LITTLE GIRL DESTINY" THING TO YOURSELF. I'VE BEEN KICKED IN THE BALLS ENOUGH TODAY.

OKAY, YOU JUMPED FROM A HELICOPTER TO GET HERE. THINK.
BUSINESSWOMAN WON'T GET ME ANYWHERE.
GOT A GODDAMNED MASTERS IN INVESTIGATIVE JOURNALISM AND TWO EMMYS...
...AND I GOTTA ROCK A WET T-SHIRT TO BREAK A STORY.
OYE, CHICA! SLOW THAT SHIT DOWN! WHATCHOO THINK, MIJO? SHE A COP?
DOMINICAN
DON'T KNOW. DON'T CARE. HEY BABY...
I'M WITH KLA. I WANNA TALK TO THE GUY IN CHARGE.
KLA 8 NEWS

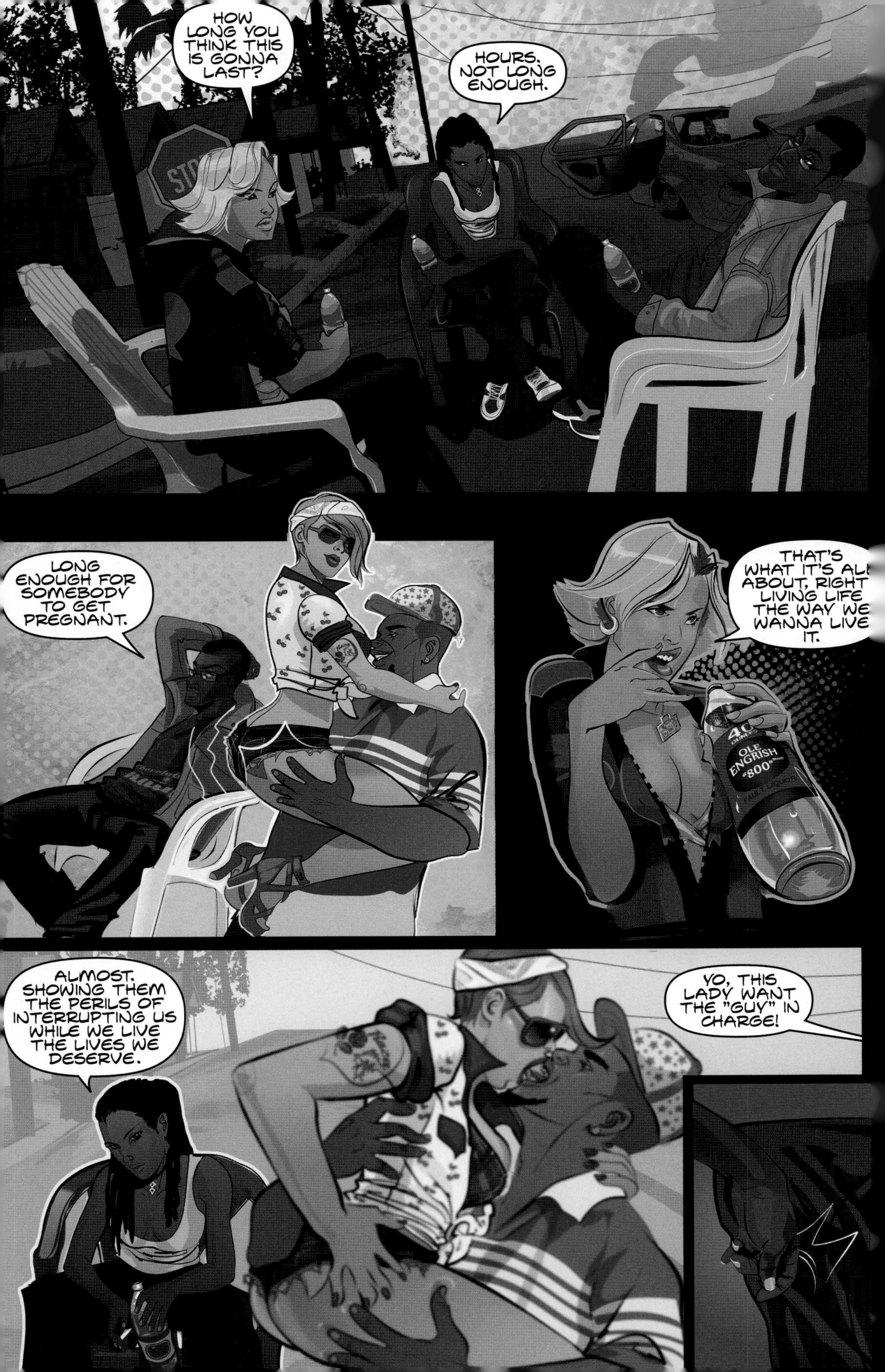
HOW LONG YOU THINK THIS IS GONNA LAST?
HOURS. NOT LONG ENOUGH.
LONG ENOUGH FOR SOMEBODY TO GET PREGNANT.
THAT'S WHAT IT'S ALL ABOUT, RIGHT LIVING LIFE THE WAY WE WANNA LIVE IT.
40 OUNCE OLE ENGRISH "800" BRAND MALT LIQUOR
ALMOST. SHOWING THEM THE PERILS OF INTERRUPTING US WHILE WE LIVE THE LIVES WE DESERVE.
YO, THIS LADY WANT THE "GUY" IN CHARGE!

RIGHT HERE. WATCHOO WANT, BITCH? YOU LOOKING TO GET KILLT?! OR YOU WANT SUM 'A THIS?
I WANT TWO THINGS. FIRST, I WANT TO INTERVIEW THE PERSON RUNNING THIS REVOLUTION.
AND, SECOND, I WANT TO KNOW WHY *SHE* THOUGHT *YOU* COULD FIT THAT BILL.

SO... WE'RE JUST SUPPOSED TO WATCH?
THAT'S THE WORD FROM THE GOVERNOR.
OF COURSE, THAT DOESN'T MEAN WE HAVE TO SIT ON OUR HANDS.
POLICE

NO, SIR. NO IT DOESN'T.
HANDLE IT.

GERALD, RUN ANOTHER CAMERA SWEEP. MAKE SURE THEY'RE ALL UP AND RUNNING FOR WHEN THIS IDYLL ENDS.
HE'S SMARTER THAN ANY TEN PEOPLE YOU COULD PUT IN A ROOM. PUT TOGETHER.
HOW DID YOU KNOW?
THOSE WORDS WERE LIKE MARBLES IN HIS MOUTH.
AND FROM THE MOMENT I APPROACHED, ALL EYES WERE ON YOU. I'M A REPORTER. I NOTICE THINGS.
AND YOU MADE IT THROUGH THE GUARDS PRETTY EASILY.
I'M SURE YOU CAN FIGURE OUT HOW.
IF THEY AREN'T THINKING WITH ONE GUN IT'S THE OTHER.

AND YOU WANT SOMETHING.
YOUR GIRL HERE IS A PULITZER WAITING TO HAPPEN. I WANT AN INTERVIEW. CLEARLY, I'LL DO WHATEVER IT TAKES TO GET IT -- I ALREADY JUMPED OUT OF A HELICOPTER.
FOLLOW ME. BRING YOUR CAMERA. WHATEVER YOU GET, YOU DON'T AIR UNTIL THIS IS OVER. EMBARGOED.
YO, LEMME GET ONE OF THEM BURGERS. YOU GOT CHEESE?
YOU COOL, ALONZO. WE ALL THINK IT, MAN. BUT YOU AIN'T BLED, YOU AIN'T FED.
JACK ASSSS
ALL TH' TIME
Old No.7 BRAND
Tennessee
WHISKEY

OYE, ELCOME TO THE FIGHT.
USED TIRES
YOU BITCHES HAVE FUN ON YO' LITTLE WALK?
BLD 420
WAY TO MISS EVERYTHING.

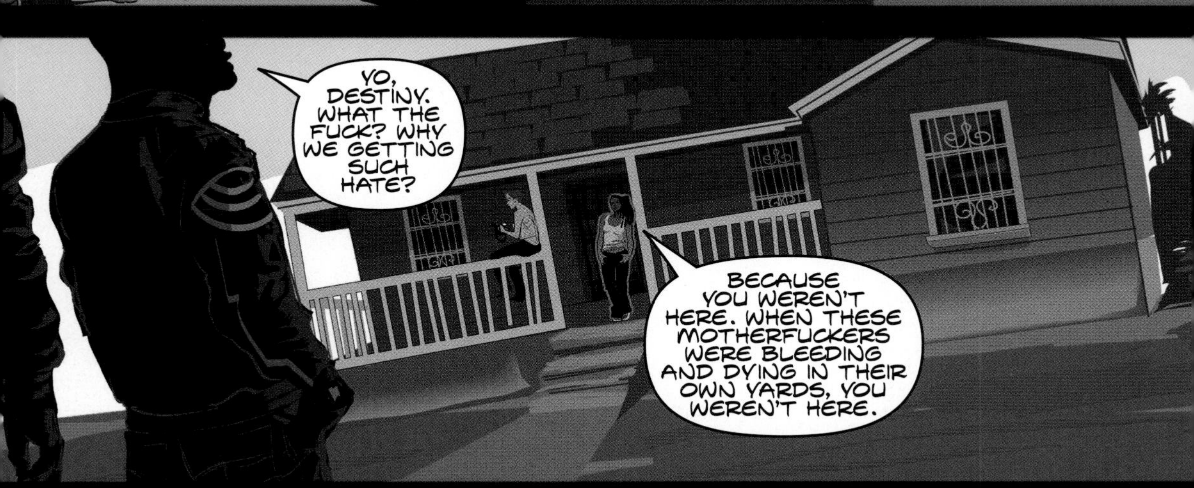
YO, DESTINY. WHAT THE FUCK? WHY WE GETTING SUCH HATE?
BECAUSE YOU WEREN'T HERE. WHEN THESE MOTHERFUCKERS WERE BLEEDING AND DYING IN THEIR OWN YARDS, YOU WEREN'T HERE.

BUT YOU SENT US. YOU TOLD US YOU NEEDED US TO RECRUIT. SO WE DID. AND NOW WE THE ASSHOLES?

TOUGH SHIT. YOUR MISSION KEPT YOU ALIVE. THEY'LL GET OVER IT.
BUT YOU'RE BAD FOR MORALE RIGHT NOW. SO GO RELIEVE CAMARO. GUARD THE LINES FOR A BIT.

WE GOT YOU, MAN. GO ON AND KICK IT. ONE OF US SHOULD.
THE PIGS ON THE OTHER SIDE AIN'T NOTHING, MAN. THEY JUS' STANDING THERE.

WATCHOO GOT, CABRÓN?
ALL TH' TIME
Old No.7 BRAND
Jennessee
WHISKEY

POLICE
GET SOME.

TEN YEARS AGO. A LITTLE GIRL WATCHES HER PARENTS GET GUNNED DOWN BY THE POLICE.
DESTINY AJAYE.
I WAS THERE. I PROCESSED THE SCENE. I COULD'VE HELPED. I SHOULD'VE...
IS SHE...IS ALL THIS *MY FAULT?*
DATE
SS#
Ajaye,Destiny
Case# 07BD-2k19-11
Notes:

THIS IS BULLSHIT. I'M HUNGRY.
WE GOOD?
OH, WE GOOD.
YOU REMEMBER WHAT THAT SWAT DUDE SAID...

"GET SOME."
QUALITEE
SOWAH MASHUP
WHISKEY

CHAPTER FOUR

IF THEY CAN'T DO IT FROM THE OUTSIDE, WE'VE GOTTA DO IT FROM THE INSIDE.
LET'S PUT AN END TO THIS SHIT.
UCKY TRIX
Good Enough
Whole Grrz-ain!
Enjoy!

THIS IS JUST GONNA BE US--I'D HOPE THAT SWAT WILL HEAR HELL BREAKING LOOSE AND COME IN, BUT WE CAN'T COUNT ON IT. SO WE HAVE TO DO THIS RIGHT.
WE CAN'T COMPETE WITH DESTINY FOR EITHER MANPOWER OR FIREPOWER.
OR BRAINPOWER. THAT BITCH IS CRAZY SMART, MAN.
NO SHIT. BUT SHE'S NOT A FUCKING PSYCHIC. THE ONLY THING WE'VE GOT IS SURPRISE.
DESTINY WILL BE IN HER HOUSE...HERE. SHE MAY BE THROWING A PARTY, BUT SHE DON'T PARTY.
GO BY TWOS. WE NEED MEN HERE...HERE... AND HERE.
D's CRIB
BE IN YOUR POSITIONS BY 1:55, BECAUSE WE'RE GOING AT 2. THE CIVVIES ARE GONE SO THE ONLY PEOPLE YOU'LL HIT ARE ENEMY COMBATANTS.
BUT WE KNOW SOME OF THESE GUYS, MAN.
YEAH, WE DO. SO SHOOT TO KILL. YOU DON'T WANN HAVE TO LISTEN TO THEM BEG FOR THEIR LIVES.
THIS IS WHAT IT MEANS TO B UNDERCOVER SOMETIMES YOU HAVE TO BURN IT ALL DOWN. LET'S GO.

AND COVER THOSE BADGES UP.
I TOL' YOU, I AIN'T GIVING YOU SHIT.
I DON'T WANT YOUR CRUSTY-ASS BURGERS, MAN.
STOP
THREE...
TWO...
ONE...

BUDDABUDDABUDDA
BUDDABUDD
BRAKKA BRAKKA
BRAKKA
BRAKKA

WHAT THE HELL IS GOING ON IN THERE?
NOT OUR BUSINESS, MAN. THEY DON'T SHOOT AT US, WE DON'T GIVE A SHIT. LET 'EM THIN THEIR OWN HERD.
SON F A TCH!
DAMN.

GERALD, IS THERE ANYONE ON COMMS?
GERALD! I NEED EYES!
V-YEAH. OKAY. I THIN CUTLASS SQUAD WASN PARTYING. THEY'RE NEXT DOOR
WAKE UP, GIRL. IT'S TIME FOR YOU TO GO. YOU GOT WHAT YOU WANTED. REMEMBER OUR DEAL: NONE OF THAT INTERVIEW AIRS UNTIL THIS IS OVER.
YOU FOUND YOUR WAY IN, YOU CAN FIND YOUR WAY OUT.
I NEED YOU, GERALD. FOCUS. SEE IF YOU CAN FIND CHAVONNE.
IF YOU'RE ON, SOUND OFF. WHO'S UP AND ABLE?
GERALD, IT'S ALONZO AND HIS BOYS. PULL THEIR FACES FROM THE CAMERAS AND BLAST TO EVERYONE'S CELL.
WE GOTTA PUSH BACK, AND WE GOTTA DO IT NOW.

ALONZO, YOU BITCH! I'M COMING FOR YOU!
SEAL THE EXITS! NO WAY OUT, PUTA!
BLAM
WHERE WERE YOU?
FUCKING SOME GUY. HEY, IT WAS A PARTY.
YEAH. IT WAS.
GERALD, I THINK THERE'S AT LEAST ONE MORE. DO YOU HAVE ANYONE ELSE ON CAMERA?
FINE. "G-TRON." ARE YOU THERE?
BRRAAAP
GERALD?
LOOKEE WHO WE FOUND, DESTINY! WHAT YOU WANNA DO WITH HIM?
WHAT ARE YOU GONNA DO WITH ME? TRADE ME BACK TO THE COPS FOR SOME CONCESSION? SHOOT ME IN COLD BLOOD?
I'VE DONE A LOT OF KILLING TODAY, ALONZO. BUT YOU'RE THE ONLY ONE WHO GOT MY BLOOD HOT.
SO, YEAH. I'M GONNA KILL YOU.

SOMEBODY DRAG THIS MOTHERFUCKER TO THE COLD HOUSE. OR NOT, I DON'T CARE.
LOS ANGELES POLICE
PARTY'S OVER. MAN YOUR POSTS.
GERALD, YOU CAN'T GO DROPPING OUT ON ME LIKE THAT...
...I EEDED YOU.
NO...

YOU BEEN IN HERE A WHILE, DEE. YOU OKAY?
NO.
HE'S DEAD, CHAVONNE, AND I CAN'T EVEN BURY HIM RIGHT.
OFFLINE

WAS THAT AN UNCOMFORTABLE SILENCE?
I'LL TAKE ALL THE SILENCE I CAN GET.

WITHOUT GERALD, WE'VE LOST OUR EYES. WE CAN'T GET CAUGHT WITH OUR PANTS DOWN AGAIN. WE NEED INFORMATION.
HELP ME CARRY HIS BODY. THEN WE NEED TO DO THAT THING I HATE.

GIVE HIM A HOUSE BETTER THAN HIS HOUSE AND A FAMILY BETTER THAN HIS FAMILY...

YOU KNOW YOU CAN'T GO IN THERE SMELLING LIKE CRIP AND GUNPOWDER, GIRL, SO STOP COMPLAINING.
NOT THAT THIS IS, IN ANY WAY, A GOOD IDEA.

NO, BUT IT'S THE ONLY IDEA I'VE GOT LEFT.

YOU'RE GONNA HAVE TO KEEP THEM IN LINE WHILE I'M GONE.

THOSE ARE GONNA HURT.
YES, BUT YOU GOT NO CHOICE. PUT 'EM ON AND SHUT UP.

THIS CAN WORK.
IT'S CALLED SOCIAL ENGINEERING.
IF YOU FORCE YOUR APPROPRIATENESS UPON PEOPLE WITH MATTER-OF-FACT CONVICTION, MORE OFTEN THAN NOT, THEY'LL ACCEPT THAT YOU BELONG.
IN OTHER WORDS, YOU GOTTA TALK THE TALK AND WALK THE WALK.
ELES POLICE DEPARTMENT

USELESS.
I'VE BEEN SITTING ON THIS INFORMATION FOR YEARS AND WHEN IT MATTERED, IT DIDN'T COUNT FOR A GODDAMNED THING.
NO, DON'T GET UP. I SEE YOU'RE BUSY.
BUSY AS I EVER WAS, CAPTAIN. THINKING UP SHIT THAT DIDN'T MATTER.
NOT TRUE, REGGIE. YOU SAVED SOME LIVES TODAY.
AREN'T YOU THE ONE WHO KEEPS SAYING THAT INFORMATION IS THE ONLY WEAPON WE NEED? WELL, YOU KEPT US LOADED.
IT'S NOT YOUR FAULT WE DIDN'T KNOW HOW TO AIM.
ANYWAY, IT'S OUT OF OUR HANDS, NOW.
WHAT DO YOU MEAN?
THE NATIONAL GUARD IS ON ITS WAY. AND THEY'RE ROLLING HEAVY.
USELESS.

COURAGE, GIRL.
NO, I'M HERE TO SEE CAPTAIN HARDY. SELA JAMESON FROM THE MADRASA INSTITUTE.
I DON'T SEE YOU HERE.
LOOK AGAIN.
SOME DAYS, RIGHT? IT'S AS IF THEY DON'T THINK I BELONG HERE.
IT'S HIS JOB. KEEPING THE WRONG PEOPLE OUT.
WE'LL SEE HOW GOOD HE IS AT IT.
AND WHO ARE YOU?
IAD. AND I'D WATCH YOUR TONE, SERGEANT. I'M HAVING A VERY SHITTY DAY.
WALK IT. TALK IT. BE THOU NOT AFRAID.

SURE, I COULD'VE POSED AS A JANITOR OR A SECRETARY, BUT IT WOULDN'T HAVE GRANTED ME THE ACCESS I NEED.
PLUS, NO ONE WANTS TO BE TOO NEAR TO INTERNAL AFFAIRS FOR TOO LONG. WE'RE TOXIC.
AREN'T YOU A LITTLE SHORT FOR INTERNAL AFFAIRS? AND A LITTLE YOUNG?
NOT SO SHORT OR YOUNG THAT I CAN'T HAVE YOUR ASS BOUNCED FROM ACTIVE DUTY TO CATALOGING EVIDENCE IN FRESNO JUST BECAUSE *I FUCKING FEEL LIKE IT.*
CONFIDENTIAL
RESPOND TO A CHALLENGE TO YOUR AUTHORITY WITH A CLAIM TO GREATER AUTHORITY.
HMM. SOMEBODY ELSE THAT NO ONE IS TALKING TO.

THIS IS AN AWFUL LOT OF TINDER.
USED TO BE RESEARCH. GOD, USED TO BE MY LIFE.
WHO ARE YOU?
INTERNAL AFFAIRS. WHAT HAPPENED?
DETECTIVE REGINALD GREY
WHAT HAPPENED? TODAY HAPPENED. A TEENAGED GIRL DECLARED WAR AGAINST THE LAPD AND KICKED THEIR COLLECTIVE ASSES.
OUR ASSES. YOU STILL WORK HERE, RIGHT?
LOOKS LIKE YOU WERE ON TO SOMETHING. WALK ME THROUGH IT.
YOU TELL ME. ACTUALLY, I DON'T CARE. I COULD'VE STOPPED ALL OF THIS, IF ONLY THEY'D LISTENED TO ME.
DESTINY
HOLY SHIT.
HOLY SHIT.

IT ALL MADE SENSE. I KNEW WHAT WAS HAPPENING IN THE GANG COMMUNITY. THE CONSOLIDATION OF POWER. THE CONDITIONS WERE RIGHT FOR THIS SORT OF THING.
I DIDN'T KNOW SHE WAS A KID UNTIL I WENT TO THE DMZ MYSELF.
SUSPECT ZERO??
DECEASED
RUNNERS
REALLY? AND YOU MADE IT BACK? IMPRESSIVE.

LUCKY IS MORE LIKE IT.
BUT WHAT I DON'T GET IS WHY.

YOU KNOW WHY. YOU KNOW WHAT IT'S LIKE IN THE HOOD. I CAN TELL BY ALL OF THIS YOU DO.
NO, NOT THAT... IT'S JUST. WHY?

...FUCK IT.

MAYBE THERE ISN'T A WHY. OR WORSE, MAYBE THERE IS AND SHE IMPLY DOESN'T KNOW IT... ONLY THAT SHE'S VERY GOOD AT BREAKING THINGS.
WHAT IF YOU WERE *SO* GOOD AT A THING THAT HAD NO APPLICATION IN A CIVILIZED WORLD?
WOULDN'T THAT FRUSTRATE YOU TO THE POINT WHERE YOU'D ORCHESTRATE YOUR LIFE TO FIND SOME WAY TO SATISFY THAT? SO THAT A HINT OF FRICTION WOULD LIGHT THE FIRE?
DECEASED
DECEASED
AND FIRE IS WHAT YOU'RE AFTER IF ALL YOU WANT IS TO WATCH THE WORLD BURN. MAYBE IF SHE COULD CHANGE THINGS AT THE SAME TIME, IT'D FEEL LESS SELFISH. LESS...EMPTY. LIKE THROWING A FIRECRACKER DOWN A WELL.
DOESN'T MATTER ANYMORE. THE NATIONAL GUARD IS ON THEIR WAY. TANKS. APCS. THE WHOLE DEAL. IN AN HOUR, IT'LL ALL BE OVER.
BUT IT WAS NICE TO TALK TO SOMEONE WHO GETS IT.
NICE TO MEET YOU, DETECTIVE GRAY. I GOTTA BE SOMEWHERE. DESTINY CALLS.

HMM. ROUGH HANDS. STRANGE FOR IAD...AND THAT CUT...
AJAYE, DESTINY
SON OF A...
SHE WAS RIGHT HERE. DESTINY.
EXIT

CHAVONNE! YOU NEED TO GET EVERYONE UP AND ON THE LINE! THE NATIONAL GUARD IS COMING!

STANDARD PEACEKEEPING DEPLOYMENT CALLS FOR APACHES AND TANKS. I DON'T KNOW HOW MANY. I'M ON MY WAY.
B1
KEY STATI
CAN I HELP YOU, LADY?
FWIP
ACK GHRGLE.
SKREECH

POLICE

CHAPTER FIVE

THERE COMES A TIME IN EVERY MILITARY CAMPAIGN WHEN IT'S CLEAR THAT VICTORY IS NO LONGER WITHIN YOUR GRASP.

10

Los Angeles
WHEN ALL YOU CAN DO IS TRY AND LIMIT THE COLLATERAL DAMAGE.
POLICE
108
WHEN YOU'RE GOOD AND TRULY FUCKED.
THE THING IS...THAT' WHERE THIS STARTE THERE WAS NO WINNI THIS. JUST LOSING. WITH PURPOSE.

I MIGHT'VE TAUGHT MYSELF TO FIELD-STRIP AN M-16, BUT I ONLY EVER READ THE HOW TO RIDE A MOTORCYCLE BOOK ONCE.
OKAY, I SKIMMED.
POLICE
108
POLICE
THE ABRAMS TOPS OUT AT 45 MPH. WHICH IS FAST ENOUGH THAT I'VE GOTTA SLOW 'EM DOWN.
I NEED ROAD BLOCKS.

OPEN UP!
84 DOWNTOWN LA
POLICE
WHAT THE HELL?
I'M GONNA NEED YOU TO GO BACK WITH THE PASSENGERS. I'LL ONLY BE A MOMENT.
I JUST PLANTED A BOMB ON THIS BUS. IT'S GOT A MOTION TRIGGER. ANYONE GETS OUTTA THEIR SEAT, YOU ALL DIE!
I NEED THEM TO STAY C
THE BUS. IF THEY RUN
THIS DOESN'T WORK.
IT'S ON THE GUARD, NOW. HOW MUCH DO THEY WANT IT?
POLICE
DAMNIT
FIND ME
ANOTHE
ROUTE

WHAT'S GOING ON, OFFICERS?
WE'RE PULLING OUT. LET THOSE FUCKING ANIMALS HAVE IT. FOR NOW.
4 BALL
M27 LINK
1C-0OL692L080
YOU BEST TURN YO ASS AROUND, BITCH. LESS'N YOU WANNA GET DEAD.
WHAT DID I SAY ABOUT THAT SHIT, TYRELL?
DAMN, GIRL. YOU CLEAN UP GOOD. LIKE SOME TYLER PERRY SHIT.
TELL EVERYONE TO GET THEIR GUNS AND BE AT MY PLACE IN FIVE. WHERE'S CHAVONNE? AND MY GODDAMN BOOTS!

IF YOU ASKED ME THREE DAYS AGO HOW THIS SHIT WAS GONNA GO DOWN, I WOULD NOT HAVE SAID WE'D SEND THE COPS RUNNING.
JUST BEIN' HONEST.
BUT THEY'RE NOT LEAVING BECAUSE WE WON. THEY'RE LEAVING BECAUSE THEY'RE GETTING REPLACED. BY SOMETHING WE CAN'T BEAT.
THE NATIONAL GUARD.
BUT WE CAN SLOW 'EM DOWN. WE CAN MAKE 'EM HURT. WE CAN PRIVATE RYAN THEIR ASSES.
MR. PHILLIP HAS THA ROOFIN TAR BEHI HIS HOUS SOMEON GET IT.
CHARGER AND FLEETWOOD, YOU GET ON THE LINE. CHAVONNE, YOU TAKE CUTLASS AND PREP THE BACK DOOR.
THUNDERBIRD, YOU'RE WITH ME.
THE BACK DOOR?
THIS WILL NOT GO WELL, CHAVONNE. WE'RE AT THE END OF IT. AND WE BOTH HAVE OUR ROLES TO PLAY BEFORE IT'S DONE.

DON'T PUT THE FUSE IN UNTIL AFTER YOU DIP. AFTER YOU LIGHT 'EM, YOU'LL ONLY HAVE A FEW SECONDS.
DRE, YOU AND TY GO DOWN HERE. BOBBY, YOU AND TRAIN UP ON THE LEFT.
HOW LONG DO YOU THINK, DEE?
MINUTES, MAYBE. YOU GOT YOUR LIGHTER?
DESTINY...?

WHY AIN'T THIS WORKING, DEE?
JUST RELAX, MAN. IT'LL LIGHT WHEN IT HAS TO LIGHT.
WE NOT MAKING IT OUTTA HERE, ARE WE, DEE?
JUST RELAX.
SEE?
NO. WE ARE NOT MAKING IT OUT OF HERE.
RUUUMMB

IT'S NOT ENOUGH. NOWHERE NEAR ENOUGH.
KLA-B-BOOM

YOU DID GOOD BACK THERE. YOU SHOULD BE PROUD. GO ON BACK TO YOUR SQUAD.
YES, MA'AM.
OKAY, WE DO THIS LIKE THE FIRST DAY. THEY'RE GOING TO COME AT US FROM THE NORTH AND THE EAST.
DON'T RUSH. DON'T WASTE YOUR BULLETS. DON'T FORGET WHY WE'RE HERE.
AND MAKE THEM REMEMBER WHAT HAPPENS WHEN THEY ROLL IN TO OUR HOME UNINVITED.
ADAM VS THE MAN
COPS WERE ONE THING, BUT THE NATIONAL GUARD? WE'RE NOT GONNA LAST LONG.
THE BACK DOOR IS READY. HOW LONG SHOULD I WAIT?
YOU'LL KNOW WHEN.
GOD, I LOVE YOU SO MUCH, CHAVONNE. YOU'RE THE LAST OF--
SHHHH. YOU JUST WATCH YOUR NARROW ASS DEE. AND CO BACK TO ME OKAY?

S THIS WHAT CUSTER FELT? LEONIDAS? SHAKA ZULU?
KNOWING FULL WELL THAT YOU DON'T STAND A CHANCE, THAT NO AMOUNT OF BATTLEFIELD TRICKERY WOULD WIN THE DAY?
WERE THEY THIS AT PEACE?

HERE WE GO! HOLD YOUR POSITIONS!

BRRAAK
NO, THIS WON'T LAST LONG.
OUTNUMBERED AND OUTGUNNED.
HIT 'EM!
CHAVONNE, IT'S TIME.
THUNDERBIRD, YOU'RE WITH ME!

REMEMBER WHEN I SAID BATTLEFIELD TRICKERY WOULDN'T HELP?

I MIGHT'VE LIED. JUST A LITTLE.

PA-FWISHH

SMOKE GRENADE! SWITCH TO THERMAL!

THESE'RE USELESS!

IT'S HOT TODAY. A HUNDRED DEGREES, MAYBE. HOT ENOUGH TO MAKE US INVISIBLE. BUT NOT FOR LONG.
CHAVONNE! LEAD 'EM OUT!

GUNS IN THE ACID, THE RIDES ARE A BLOCK AWAY. MOVE!
THUNDERBIRD, WE NEED TO MAKE IT LOOK LIKE WE'RE ALL STILL HERE. FILL THE HOLES WHERE YOU CAN.
HOLD THE LINE.
SACRIFICE IS WHAT MAKES WARFARE WORK. WITHOUT IT, VICTORY IS IMPOSSIBLE.
I WOULD DIE FOR ANY OF THESE MEN. THEY'VE EARNED IT.
BUT I CAN DO MORE FOR THEM IF I LIVE.

YEAH, I'M RUNNING AWAY.
IT WAS ALWAYS PART OF THE PLAN.
BUT, SOMETIMES, THE PLAN CURDLES IN YOUR STOMACH LIKE RANCID MILK.
HELLO, 911. THIS IS DESTINY AJAYE. SINCE YESTERDAY MORNING, I KILLED ABOUT 90 POLICEMEN. PROBABLY MORE.
I NEED TO TALK TO DETECTIVE GRAY AND CAPTAIN HARDY...

TELL THEM I'M RIGHT OUTSIDE.
POLICE
POLICE DEPARTMENT
POLICE

ABOUT TIME. IT'S GETTING HOT IN THIS THING.
THIS SHIT AIN'T FUNNY, LADY, AND I AIN'T IN A JOKING MOOD.
ME NEITHER. I'M HERE TO DISCUSS THE TERMS OF MY SURRENDER.
I'VE HEARD THE RADIO CHATTER. YOUR REBELLION IS OVER. THE GUARD SQUASHED IT.
WAIT FOR THE CASUALTY REPORTS. THEY'LL TELL YOU THAT THEY FOUND MAYBE A DOZEN GANGBANGER BODIES.
YOU WERE THERE. YOU KNOW HOW MANY MEN I HAD. ASK YOURSELVES: WHERE'D THEY ALL GO?
POLICE
IF I DON'T GET WHAT I WANT, THEN THIS WAR IS FAR FROM OVER. I COULD RUN IT FROM PRISON AS EASILY AS I DID FROM THE STREET. JUST LIKE THE PCC DID IN BRAZIL.
AND THE WAR ZONE WOULDN'T BE TWO BLOCKS OF SOUTH CENTRAL. IT'D BE THE WHOLE DAMNED CITY.

I COULD BRING THIS CITY TO ITS KNEES WITH A CELL PHONE.
SO, WHAT DO YOU WANT?
A CEASEFIRE. AND AMNESTY FOR MY MEN. NO APBS. NO MOST-WANTED LISTS.
BESIDES, I'M THE ONE YOU WANT. I'M THE ONE THAT GETS YOU THE PROMOTION. I'M THE ONE THAT GETS THE MAYOR RE-ELECTED.
ARREST ME. PUT ME AWAY. BUT ONLY ME.
TAKE THE DEAL, BOSS.
I CAN'T MAKE THAT CALL, REGGIE. IT'S *WAY* ABOVE MY PAY GRADE.
BUT NOT ABOVE MINE.
ON BEHALF OF THE UNITED STATES GOVERNMENT AND THE MADRASA INSTITUTE I ACCEPT THOSE TERMS.
THE KILLING STOPS?
YES. NO MANHUNTS?
YES. AND WE'RE DONE HERE.
GOOD. THIS MUCH PLAY-DOH IS HEAVY.

I GOTTA SAY, I'M NOT FAMILIAR WITH YOUR PARTICULAR BRANCH OF THE GOVERNMENT.
YOU'RE NOT SUPPOSED TO BE. THAT'S THE WHOLE IDEA.
EVEN SOMEONE WITH SUCH EXEMPLARY PATTERN RECOGNITION SKILLS AS YOURSELF WOULD HAVE A HARD TIME FINDING IT.
I'VE READ YOUR NOTES, DETECTIVE GRAY. THE FACT THAT YOU WERE THE ONLY PERSON TO CORRECTLY IDENTIFY THE THREAT HASN'T ESCAPED ME.
WE COULD ALWAYS USE SOMEONE LIKE YOU. IF YOU WANT TO MAKE MORE AND GET SHOT AT LESS.
WHAT'LL HAPPEN TO HER?
IF YOU WANT TO KNOW WHAT'LL BECOME OF DESTINY AJAYE, COME WORK FOR ME. IF NOT: CLASSIFIED.

DURING THE SIEGE OF SOUTH CENTRAL THAT ENDED THREE DAYS AGO, I WAS LUCKY ENOUGH TO SIT DOWN WITH DESTINY AJAYE, THE ARCHITECT OF THOSE EVENTS.
SHE AGREED TO AN INTERVIEW ON THE CONDITION THAT IT WOULDN'T AIR UNTIL THE SIEGE WAS OVER. THIS IS ISABEL CORTINA PRESENTING A KLAP EXCLUSIVE.

KLA NEWS 8

SOUTH CENTRAL UNDER SEIGE
EXCLUSIVE INTERVIEW

THE QUESTION THAT EVERYONE WILL WANT TO KNOW IS "WHY?"
AND THAT'S THE WRONG QUESTION TO ASK. "WHY" SHOULD BE CLEAR TO ANYONE WHO'S BEEN PAYING ATTENTION TO THE WORLD AROUND THEM.

NO. THE QUESTION YOU SHOUL BE ASKING IS "WHEN"? WHEN WILL HAPPEN IN NEIGHBORHOO WHEN WILL T SAY "I'VE HA ENOUGH"?
CIVILIZATION IS NOTHING BU A COLLECTION AGREEMENTS MADE BETWEE PEOPLE TO WO TOGETHER TOWARDS A COMMON GOAL.

HOW LONG BEFORE PEOPLE FEEL LIKE THOSE AGREEMENTS AREN'T IN THEIR BEST INTEREST?

ORDER IS ALWAYS ONE REALIZATION AWAY FROM DISINTEGRATION.
WHAT DO YOU THINK IS GOING TO HAPPEN TO YOU WHEN YOU'RE DONE?

HEH. IF I SURVIVE...?

"OH, I THINK THEY'RE GOING TO LOCK ME UP FOR A LONG, LONG TIME."
"THEY WILL STICK ME IN A HOLE..."
MADRASA
STITUTE
Operation Overlord
Code name: D-Day
"...FAR AWAY FROM EVERYTHING AND EVERYONE."
"YOU'LL PROBABLY NEVER SEE ME AGAIN."
UNTIL I'VE LEARNED EVERYTHING THEY HAVE TO TEACH. UNTIL MY MIND IS RAZOR-SHARP.
UNTIL I'M READY.
THE END.

Minotaur Press,
a Top Cow productions company,
presents...

Bonus Preview

Matt Hawkins
Co-creator & writer

Rahsan Ekedal
Co-creator & artist

Bill Farmer
Colorist

Troy Peteri
Letterer

Special thanks to Linda Sejic
for The Tithe logo design.

rvine, California
:20 AM Sunday
THE TREASURES OF THIS EARTH ARE TRANSITORY, MEANINGLESS, AND DESPITE THE PLENTY GOD HAS *GIFTED* US WITH, THERE ARE STILL THOSE WHO LACK THEIR BASIC NEEDS. OUR CHURCH MINISTERS TO THOSE AND THE BODY OF CHRIST MUST *GIVE* CHEERFULLY AS THE LORD COMMANDS.
BEFORE WE TAKE THE COLLECTION TODAY, TAKE A MOMENT AND REFLECT ON THOSE LESS FORTUNATE AND GIVE WHAT YOU CAN. ADD TO YOUR HEAVENLY ACCOUNT...*TODAY.*
LET US PRAY. OUR HEAVENLY FATHER, WE COME BEFORE YOU WITH AN OPEN HEART. WE'RE THANKFUL OF THE BOUNTY YOU'VE GRACED US WITH...
...AND KNOW THE RIGHT THING IS TO GIVE BACK TO YOUR MINISTRY SO YOU CAN USE THE CHURCH TO MEET THE NEEDS OF SO MANY. AMEN.

ARE YOU FILLED WITH THE GRACE OF GOD? LET'S SING AND GIVE PRAISE WHILE THE USHERS MOVE UP AND DOWN THE AISLES TO GIVE YOU THE OPPORTUNITY TO GIVE BACK TO GOD FROM WHAT HE HAS GIVEN TO YOU.
♪ALL TO JESUS I SURRENDER, ALL TO HIM I FREELY GIVE;♪
♪I WILL EVER LOVE AND TRUST HIM, IN HIS PRESENCE DAILY LIVE.♪
♪I SURRENDER ALL,♪
♪I SURRENDER ALL,♪
♪I SURRENDER ALL,♪
♪I SURRENDER ALL,♪
♪ALL TO THEE, MY BLESSED SAVIOR,♪
♪I SURRENDER ALL.♪

Mom's Flowers
SCREEEEEEEE
JESUS#1
WOOHOO, KYLE! LET'S KICK SOME ASS.
NO NAMES, IDIOT.
STAY CLOSE.
AUTHORIZING PASSCODE
UNLOCKING...
SMILE FOR THE CAMERA.

SHOULD BE ONE GUARD.
ON THE GROUND! NOW!
IS THAT SINGING?
♪I SURRENDER ALL,♪
YEAH.
RESTRICTED ACCESS
AUDITORIUM
FIRE DOOR MUST REMAIN CLOSED
JUST BE COOL. WE DON'T WANT TO HURT ANYONE.
HOW LONG?
LEMME ASK SAMARITAN.
AUDITORIUM
FIRE DOOR MUST REMAIN CLOSED
I THOUGHT YOU SAID NO NAMES?
Unknown
2 minutes
DID YOU WATCH THE VIDEO, DUMB ASS?

ISN'T IT GREAT TO BE A CHRISTIAN? CAN I GET AN AMEN?
AMEN!
AMEN!
AMEN!

OPEN YOUR BIBLES TO LUKE CHAPTER SIXTEEN.

MORE THAN EARLY SERVICE.

THAT'S UNUSUAL. EARLY SKEWS OLDER, THEY USUALLY GIVE MORE.

LET'S GET IT TO THE COUNTING ROOM. JAY, IF YOU CAN STAY AND HELP ME WITH THE COUNT, I'D APPRECIATE IT.

OF COURSE. HAPPY TO BE OF SERVICE.

HANDS UP, ALL OF YOU!
AUDITORIUM
FIRE DOOR MUST REMAIN CLOSED
DON'T BE A HERO.
UNLESS YOU WANT TO MEET YOUR GOD TODAY.
THE LORD GIVETH.
AND WE TAKETH AWAY.
JUST TAKE THE MONEY AND GO. PLEASE DON'T HURT ANYONE.
THIS IS WHAT, SIXTY-K? WE WANT THE MONEY IN THE VAULT.
WHAT ARE YOU TALKING ABOUT? ALL THE MONEY IS TRANSFERRED AFTER EACH SERVICE.
WELL, JOHN TAGGERT OF 22 LOCUST LANE, FATHER OF THREE, GRANDFATHER OF SEVEN...WE BOTH KNOW THAT'S NOT TRUE, NOW DON'T WE?
WHAT DO YOU

PUT THIS ON.
I ALREADY TOLD YOU WHAT WE WANT.
THIS IS FOUR POUNDS OF C4.
AND THIS IS A REMOTE DETONATOR. ALL I HAVE TO DO IS CLICK THIS BUTTON AND YOU CAN SAY HI TO THE DEVIL...AND MY POPS WHILE YOU'RE DOWN THERE.
Arm
Disarm
Detonate
WE KNOW YOU AND PASTOR TIBBETT HAVE BEEN HIDING MONEY. OPEN THE VAULT.
IT'S TIME ACTIVATED, I CAN'T OPEN IT UNTIL NOON.
DOESN'T GOD SAY LYING IS BAD? LAST CHANCE OR I'LL JUST LEAN YOU AGAINST THE DOOR AND DETONATE THE EXPLOSIVES TO OPEN IT.
OKAY, OKAY. PLEASE. I DON'T WANT TO DIE.

TRIP AN ALARM AND THIS TURNS INTO A HOSTAGE SITUATION.
THAT WON'T END WELL FOR YOU EITHER.
HOLY SHIT.
JACKPOT!

LUKE HAS ALWAYS BEEN MY FAVORITE OF THE GOSPELS.
CHAPTER SIXTEEN VERSE TEN SAYS, "ONE WHO IS FAITHFUL IN A VERY LITTLE IS ALSO FAITHFUL IN MUCH, AND ONE WHO IS DISHONEST IN A VERY LITTLE IS ALSO DISHONEST IN MUCH."
ISN'T IT GOOD TO BE ONE OF THE FAITHFUL?
PRAISE JESUS.
THESE PEOPLE MIGHT BE FAITHFUL.
AMEN.
BUT YOU...
...YOU'RE DISHONEST.

ATTENTION SHEEP. YOUR PASTOR IS A WOLF, NOT THE SHEPHERD HE CLAIMS TO BE. HE DIVERTED TWO POINT EIGHT MILLION DOLLARS TO A CHARITY CALLED ISLAND HOPE IN THE LAST YEAR ALONE.
PASTOR TIBBETT IS A HYPOCRITE
YOUR PASTOR MILES TIBBETT
FRAUD
RETENDER
CHARLAT
SWIN
WHAT THE--
BILLED AS AN EVANGELICAL CRUSADE DELIVERING FOOD AND JESUS TO INDIGENOUS ISLAND PEOPLES, HERE'S WHAT IT REALLY DOES.
WOMANIZER
ADULTERER
SHOW ME WHAT THE LORD GAVE YOU CHILD. DON'T BE SHY.
YOU GAVE YOUR HARD-EARNED MONEY IN GOOD FAITH. LOOK AT WHERE IT'S GONE.
PROFITEER
SHUT IT DOWN.
$36 MILLION
$18 MILLION
I CAN'T, WE'RE LOCKED OUT OF THE SYSTEM.
KILL THE POWER.

THIS ISN'T THE LORD'S WORK.
Yours truly, SAMARITAN XOXO
Yours truly, SAMARITAN XOXO
IS THAT TRUE?
Yours truly, SAMARITAN XOXO
STOP BLINDLY FOLLOWING AND OPEN YOUR EYES.
OH MY GOD.
NO SIGNAL
NO SIGNAL
LET'S GET OUT OF HERE.

COVER GALLERY

ius: Pilot Season #1 Cover A
Afua Richardson

Genius #1 Cover A
by: Afua Richardson

nius #1 Cover B
: Afua Richarson

Genius #2 Cover A
by: Nelson Blake II

nius #3 Cover A
Afua Richardson

Genius #4 Cover A
by: Nelson Blake II

ius #5 Cover A
Nelson Blake II
NB2

TOP COW
PRODUCTIONS, INC.